DEATH CAME SMILI

'The only difference between me and other people,' said Gwen, 'is that I carry my sanity separately. It lives in the country, and paints, and suffers fools.' When Gwen goes to the country to visit her beloved twin sister, Elizabeth, she is found stabbed in the family home. The open verdict leaves their mentally deficient brother under suspicion, but Elizabeth refuses to accept it. Turning her back on the country, she goes to London to live in Gwen's flat. For only there, by getting under the skin of her sister's irregular life, does she believe she can uncover the real culprit.

DEATH CAME SMILING

DEATH CAME SMILING

by

Eileen Dewhurst

Dales Large Print Books
Long Preston, North Yorkshire,
BD23 4ND, England.

British Library Cataloguing in Publication Data.

Dewhurst, Eileen
Death came smiling.

A catalogue record of this book is
available from the British Library

ISBN 978-1-84262-611-5 pbk

First published in Great Britain 1975
by Robert Hale & Company

Published in Large Print 2008 by arrangement with
Eileen Dewhurst, care of Gregory & Company

Dales Large Print is an imprint of Library Magna Books Ltd.

Printed and bound in Great Britain by
T.J. (International) Ltd., Cornwall, PL28 8RW

PART ONE

GWEN

1

To punish Thomas for sitting scowling at the wall, for not helping her, Gwen said:

'I've got to go now.'

Really, there were still several moments in hand.

Thomas appeared to have no reaction. He didn't look at her. Almost angry, Gwen said:

'Thomas, why on earth do you bother?'

He turned then towards her, an action which for him was always deliberate because it was painful, her face, her body hurt him each time with their undirected vitality. Now he saw that every muscle in her face was straining. There could have been a bruise in the corner of her mouth, unless it was a shadow. There was a bruise on her thin bare arm.

'Why does one love?' Thomas asked her, turning his head away.

'Why does one love *me?*' Gwen replied, mocking his slow heavy tones. She picked up the coat and bag lying on the sofa. 'I must go.'

'Where to?'

He showed her nothing of his cringing fear of her reply.

'To Ataveh.'

She looked him steadily in the eye and he looked away again, not in time to conceal his rage.

Gwen went out of the front door, and rang for the lift. Thomas followed, pausing to spike his mood on a last look round the room which seemed to him so clear a call for help and attention. Did Gwen really like the hot, howling colours of her walls and chairs, the contorted shapes of her furniture, the jostling, persistently erotic canvases? He banged the door. He had asked her, but she never answered that sort of question.

'Don't go to this ridiculous place,' said Thomas, in the lift, forcing himself to watch her. Her face closed, but she started to shiver.

Thomas put an arm across her shoulder and looked away.

'I'm all right,' said Gwen, not unkindly, 'don't *worry,* Thomas. I'm going to see Elizabeth.' He could feel her studying him. She said, conversationally: 'I sometimes think we must be given the sort of features best able to bear our prevailing expressions. You scowl so much, Thomas, and you do it so effectively. Heavy black brows, fleshy but aggressive nose, drooping mouth.'

Usually he loved her to tease him, it meant he had momentarily caught her attention. But this time his thoughts had stayed behind.

'Elizabeth,' he said, as they crossed the lobby, 'sister Elizabeth.'

'Twin sister.'

He held the door for her, needing strength. The constant wind, funnelled day and night between the high buildings, caught them instantly. Gwen's silver-fair hair began to agitate. Thomas had pulled the lapels of her coat up round her throat by the time her own hands reached them. He said as they walked quickly away:

'You tell me you're going to see Elizabeth as if you're saying "So that's all right..."'

'That's what I am saying. Can you find a taxi?'

Thomas always could, and did. This weighed with Gwen.

'Can I drop you, Thomas?'

'Yes. Why, what is Elizabeth?'

'The rest of me. The only difference between me and other people really, Thomas, is that I carry my sanity separately. It lives in the country, and paints, and suffers fools.'

Thomas, alone with Gwen in the privacy of the cab, felt as always further from her than when they were apart. Then, at least, the next meeting lay ahead, and he could imagine that it might be more satisfactory.

He said roughly:

'You're not playing down the difference between yourself and other people, Gwen, you're playing it up. You're screaming "Look at me!" The only justification for such entreaty is talent. Have you got any?'

Or illness, he thought, perhaps she's ill. He forced himself to look at her and saw her flinch slightly. He longed to try and comfort her physically but experience made him sit still. They stared at each other, seriously and sadly, and then she smiled, her face changed so completely that he had to lean back under the astonishment of it, the sudden upward curves, the eyes from dark to light, the tight mouth wide.

'I have a talent for *you* Thomas, I must have. I've only ever prickled you, or cried on your shoulder, and here you are. Why?'

'You know why. And we're talking about you.'

'All right. And I make a good living. "The right face at the right time", as they say. Oh, and the right body.'

'That's all it is.'

'All *right*. But why ferret for talent when it works? I'd stand or fall then, to myself, by what I did.'

'Would you?' Thomas looked at her in pleased surprise. It was a feeling he had had before over Gwen, when she showed more weight and perception than he expected of her. He wondered, sometimes, if he might be loving a creation of his own.

'How do you stand to yourself, as it is?'

'Very badly. So I'm going home.'

'Home? Do you think of Elizabeth's house as your home? May I come and see you?'

The taxi slowed down. Gwen opened the door before it stopped.

'You may not. And Elizabeth's house *is* my home. I was born there. No more comments now, Thomas, if you please. Are you getting out?'

Without speaking Thomas joined her on the pavement, and paid off the taxi. He looked up at the house behind her and stood there in continued silence, contemptuous and suppliant.

'Good-bye Thomas,' said Gwen, and he inclined his body infinitesimally towards her before walking off, his shoulders hunched, his hands in his pockets.

Gwen looked after him and wished she could love him. When he wasn't there, she almost did. He would at least be a solution. To what, she wondered, throwing the question the length and breadth of the street, and having it rebound from every direction so that the place where she stood was as cramped as a cage.

This was the mood in which she had first entered the temple of Ataveh, and she turned round and ran quickly up the steps.

The temple was distinguished from its terraced neighbours, externally, merely by a small brass plaque. But behind the door was an instant expanse of tessellated floor, dimly lit from concealed sources that revealed the vaulted ceiling and left the bare circular anteroom in semi-darkness. Curtains rose and fell in several places as silent men and women came and went, moving with a religious minimum of gesture. There was a strong smell of joss sticks.

The Master stood berobed just inside the front door. His smile was superior but all-embracing. He was so tall he scarcely lifted his hands to hold them for an instant above Gwen's head.

'My child,' he murmured.

Gwen glanced up for a moment through the canopy of those long white hands, then moved on with down-bent head. She congratulated herself on an exchange of looks with the Master. She had observed that not many of the followers of Ataveh cared to raise their eyes under the Master's blessing. Her gesture held for her something of the sense of daring she had had as a child in the church of Upper Longford when, alone in a surround of bent heads, she had looked up at the elevated Host.

The last curtain fell behind Gwen and she dismissed the comparison, as vaguely painful. She was only just in time, after all. A facetted globe turned slowly in the centre of another vaulted ceiling, giving a curious illusion of movement to the white rows of palliasses and the figures that knelt at the foot of nearly every one.

Gwen threaded her way to the nearest vacant female palliasse, and knelt down. She felt tinglingly alone, as always during the approach to Ataveh. It was impossible to believe, until the moment of contact, in the violent movement which would so soon and so suddenly overtake the motionless assembled figures.

'...through whom and for whom we come together, oh Ataveh...'

Gwen, assessing her neighbours through her fingers, came back to the Master's voice.

He could not be seen. His voice came out of a sort of net shroud on a platform in front of them.

'...through whom and for whom we offer ourselves. We, men and women, flesh and blood. By what other means can we approach thy high and distant mysteries? None other, oh Ataveh, through whom and for whom we come together...'

Come together. That was why Gwen couldn't resist looking to each side of her. That was why everyone looked around, furtively, under cover of their hands.

Part of her felt troubled at this persistent egotism, this minding of who, at last, would lay hands on her in the worship of Ataveh.

And part of her laughed, detached and intact, not afraid of this or any other frantic search for meaning or distraction.

The Master was moving towards the climax.

'Come together' he was chanting hypnotically, 'come together, come together...'

Gwen in her head said suddenly, to her astonishment:

'Meekly kneeling upon your knees.'

That was from the days when 'come together' meant attending morning service in the church at Upper Longford. It didn't matter who was beside you, because your coming together then was no more than sharing the same atmosphere of gentle piety, and perhaps the same hymn book. And her neighbours were always the same, anyway: Elizabeth and Gritsy.

'Ataveh, Ataveh, we approach thee...' The Master's voice was thickening, soon he would lead the way in the lonely climax that he, as their spearhead to Ataveh, was permitted to experience in the face of the deity.

Elizabeth. Gwen hadn't seen Elizabeth for months, hadn't spoken to her or written to her. It was a funny thing, in a way. It was because they were so close to each other, two halves of a whole, that she didn't have to be in touch with Elizabeth. If harm came to Elizabeth she would know it, she would feel it.

Do you jerk in your sleep, darling, wake up with pounding pulse, when through my neighbour I worship Ataveh?

'Come together, come together...'

The Master now was all reflex, but Gwen's body was cold and still, kneeling at the end of her palliasse. If she didn't subdue her racing thoughts she didn't think she could...

'Now, my children, now!'

The man on her left was a fraction before the signal, and Gwen was, too, rolling out of his grasp even as his arms came to surround her. As she dutifully received the weight of the man on her right – was it the rep type with the nice mild eyes, or the man with the flavour of the country on him whom she never so much minded? – the hurrying spotlight caught the eyes of the neighbour she had spurned, sparked them to baleful life and made their hatred blaze. For a moment they were as brilliant as cats' eyes under headlamps.

Gwen saw their message, and was afraid. This was simply a man who had offered himself, and been rejected. There was nothing in that fierce face to suggest that he would accept his rejection as a sacrifice to Ataveh.

What would the Master counsel?

The Master would smooth things over, he would not let either of us escape his sales message. The Master is a good salesman, or why am I here? I am an intelligent woman.'

But it was not the sudden inescapable

thought that Ataveh was no more than the Master's livelihood that made Gwen flee the ritual. It was the unbearably obscene sight of the elderly spinster nearby rushing with such pathetic eagerness to meet her god.

Roughly pushing her fellow-worshipper aside, staggering to her feet, tripping over entwined recumbent couples and hearing her own sobbing in the distance, Gwen found the curtain, and the next and the next, tearing them aside. There was a priest of Ataveh in the centre of the mosaic, studying the ceiling like a waiting bodyguard, and Gwen launched herself in headlong flight to the door. It was to God she prayed that it would yield to her and it did, more slowly than if she had not been so ridiculously desperate, but in time for her to be gulping air in the street when the priest's pale, puzzled face appeared.

The bus stop was there, where she was standing, and Gwen took her place in the queue, gazing steadily at the face until it withdrew and the heavy door was shut.

She swung on to a bus, light-hearted. No more props. No more Ataveh. In a second this latest deity had ceased to exist. She had seen through him, as through so much else, but it was a woman's face which had broken the spell. Things lived or died for tiny reasons.

Gwen got down at a red light and began to

walk quickly among loitering groups round the doors of pubs and restaurants.

'Not Ataveh,' she said aloud, and found herself leaning up against a wall, laughing. Ataveh now made such a good joke that she couldn't stop laughing. And she was going to see Elizabeth. And Sammy, and Gritsy...

A man and a girl had turned into the right angle of the building where Gwen leaned, perhaps hoping to support their embraces. They stood hand in hand looking at her with open curiosity, and she smiled at them warmly as she drifted away.

She felt happy, and the slight soft movement in her bedroom as she turned on the sitting-room light brought only mild annoyance. She moved to the bedroom doorway and stood there, and the light behind her was enough to show that a man lay on the bed.

'Go home,' said Gwen, tiredly.

The man clicked a switch and surrounded himself with pink light, as private as an aureole. He moved away from the centre of the bed.

'No,' said Gwen. 'Oh, no.'

She sat down at the dressing-table and removed necklace, watch and hairpiece.

'Strip without tease,' said the man sadly, from the prop of his elbow, but not really concentrating. 'Come on, Gwen.'

'No, Rupert, go home.'

She stopped short at her dress, but used her feet to ease off her shoes and kick them aside. She turned round on the stool.

'I mean it, Rupert. Go home. I don't want you.'

'Don't you, love? Too much highflown sex? Don't you know you can't mix sex and religion?'

'I know it,' said Gwen, and from Rupert's mouth, round in a small silent 'o' of surprise, it was clear she had departed from the script. 'That's done with.'

'It is? What, has the holy master got himself arrested? Self-abuse isn't a crime, but keeping an unregistered bawdy-house is another thing.'

Gwen nodded absently.

'A load of old rubbish, eh, eh, *eh?*'

From immobility he was across the room, kneeling, holding Gwen's chin in his hand.

She smiled at him, pulling his pale spunsilk hair.

'A load of old rubbish. You know, that's a very clever, original description of Ataveh and the Master. What's more it's accurate.'

Rupert wandered away, swinging round the room, touching things, moving on. 'Yes, and as the man said, illegal. I'm broke, by the way.'

He was beside her again, smiling at her fiercely, his hand spanning her neck. The familiar melting process began inside her, but tonight she resisted it. She got up and walked into the sitting-room.

Rupert followed her gradually. She was at her desk.

'Ten pounds,' said Gwen, tearing a cheque off. 'I'm going home, make it last.'

'Home, darling?'

'Yes, I've got roots.'

'And you're going to water them?'

'That's about it.' She looked at him with the surprised approval of Thomas for herself. He saw it and took a cat's step towards the bedroom. Gwen was flattered that, with her cheque in his pocket, he was still intent on staying. Poor Thomas, she thought, but moved ahead of Rupert and shut the bedroom door. She leaned against it.

'Go home,' she said kindly, and Rupert prowled across the room and went out, closing the front door quietly behind him. And panic rose in Gwen so that she went to sit down at her desk again, took some paper, and wrote:

'My darling girl…'

2

Elizabeth caught sight of Sammy, and began slowly to smile. She had moved to the window only out of curiosity to identify a persistently singing bird but she stayed there, settling her elbows on the sill, to watch Sammy.

He was being rewarded for his long hours of leaning on the gate, watching the lane for someone to come past so that he could smile at them and speak his few half-intelligible words. Everyone in the village knew him and stopped as they went by.

Sammy, now, was talking to a large Alsatian whose plumed tail was swinging as approvingly as Sammy's broad rear. Its handler gripped the leash, but stood by relaxed and prepared to wait while the dog and Sammy had their noses together. At one point Elizabeth caught his eye and they both nodded.

Police Constable King knew Sammy because for several months now he had been their friendly neighbourhood policeman. That was how he had described himself to Elizabeth once, inverted commas in his voice. A small photograph of him was pinned up in Upper Longford post office. Elizabeth sometimes thought about him.

When the policeman and the dog moved on she went slowly back to her painting, actively savouring her lot. She often did this, she often thought consciously that life was good. Perhaps it was because she had the daily pleasure of making a living through what she could do well and what she most enjoyed doing. And perhaps it was easiest if your talent was a small one. There was no hardship, no suffocation for Elizabeth in fulfilling her commissions for portraits and Christmas cards and dust jackets.

And anyway, there was the constant safety valve open, if she needed one (she didn't know), in the picture for her own pleasure which was always in progress. At the moment it was a portrait of Gwen, but as Elizabeth looked it in the face, the face whose gradual bruising by life she was exciting and saddening herself by capturing, she found she was wondering about other pleasures. The pleasures of her work, her independence, her home, were total – but they weren't the only ones. There was love, which Elizabeth knew of only through dreams and reading, despite the willingness she sensed in various men to enlighten her.

Gwen had known love. With Alan, Elizabeth was sure that Gwen had been in love. But then, Alan had gone suddenly from warmth to cold. Alan, with whom Gwen had over months formed thousands of small bonds, suddenly didn't want to be there. And left.

It was from this point, Elizabeth thought, as she deepened the tension of white under Gwen's eyes, that the difference between them became clear for all to see. Gwen went away, and when she came back no one ever mistook them again…

But we were always different. You always devised our fantasies, played the dashing characters, got bored and began again. I carried the ideas out, reassured us when they led to trouble, sat and listened to your impatient sighing. I wonder, do I check you sometimes darling when I lie still and alone in bed, night after night quietly sleeping?

Elizabeth didn't know any facts about Gwen's life in London, but in the few visits she had been persuaded to make she had seen strange, unwholesome men who looked as if they would wilt in daylight, heard Gwen's end of tense, unintelligible telephone conversations, never been able to hold Gwen's attention for more than the length of a cigarette. She would start to worry, and show it, and Gwen's tension would suddenly dissolve in a too boisterous laugh, Gwen (not Elizabeth) would rake up an old, utterly private joke, mention some small feature of home with perfect accuracy, and Elizabeth would be disarmed...

'El – El – Elibet!'

Sammy was in the doorway, beaming, and she ran to him, hugged him, rumpled his curls.

'Love, Elibet,' said Sammy, leaning back to admire her and smacking his lips with happiness.

'Music, Sammy?' suggested Elizabeth, and he clapped his hands.

Elizabeth switched on the transistor radio and the room was filled with pop. Sammy stood in front of the set, swaying his body, his eyes on space. He liked all music, but this with the persistent rhythm was best, and Elizabeth would let him have it until it made her head ache.

'That row!' said Mrs Grice, just loud enough for Elizabeth to hear, and good-humouredly, as she brought coffee in for Elizabeth and Sammy. She put the tray down and went to stand in front of the portrait.

'Is it going well, Elizabeth?'

'What do you think?'

Mrs Grice stood with her head on one side studying the portrait of Gwen, and Elizabeth thought 'I must paint you next.' Gritsy looked the archetypal retainer, stout and majestic-busted, very neat grey hair surrounding a rosy face. She was a country woman.

The adult presences of childhood, for

Elizabeth and Gwen, had been headed by Mrs Grice. Mother had lain on a sofa in a darkened room, ever since the accident to baby Sammy. Father, writing in his study, came jovially forth from time to time, to toss them frighteningly in the air, take them out in the car, then forget them again.

Mother was found to be dead one day when the twins tiptoed up to the sofa, one each side, to bid her good night. They thought she was asleep, as she so often was, and when they had no response to their soft kisses they looked at each other across her. Elizabeth remembered that Gwen had given a tiny shrug and recalled it as an adult gesture which even then she had seen as a sort of expression of Gwen's greater independence and sophistication.

Elizabeth had been the one to pipe: 'She keeps asleep, Gritsy!' Gwen put a deliberate hand on her cheek and said: 'Isn't she cold?'

On the safe side, Mrs Grice bustled forward and took both little girls away. Father died soon afterwards, suddenly in his office.

Elizabeth had tried not to admit to herself that she didn't miss either of her parents. What did Gwen feel? Elizabeth didn't know. They had discussed nothing of it beyond the practicalities, what would happen to them next. They had both cried, once, because Aunt Madge so clearly expected them to cry, she was so direly sorry for them.

'We're orphans!' sobbed Gwen to Mrs Grice. Mrs Grice told them to stop sniffling and lay the table for tea. They had a beautiful home, they had money, and they had her, and they must look after Sammy and be happy and good.

This, in those early days, didn't seem to be an especially difficult task for either of them, once the short time was over in which Aunt Madge moved in and got on everybody's nerves. She soon went back to her own home, and merely wrote each week to Mrs Grice.

Through all the changes, there had been Gritsy. Dear Gritsy, who was getting old. Elizabeth put her hand on Gritsy's shoulder.

'Well?'

Mrs Grice turned away from the portrait. She looked as worried as her placid face allowed. The pop programme jangled past, so far from their mood they scarcely heard it.

'Oh, Gritsy, you can't hurt *my* feelings! Just tell me if you don't like it.'

'It's a good picture, Elizabeth. It's – like her. It's – that that worries me.'

'You wish it wasn't like her?' asked Elizabeth gently.

Mrs Grice sighed. 'I believe that's what I was thinking. She isn't happy. She hasn't been happy since Alan.'

'I doubt if she was really happy before, as you and I understand it. If she'd got Alan under her belt, she'd have gone searching for the next thing.'

'Elizabeth!'

'Oh, I didn't necessarily mean another man.'

'But you really believe that, that she'd not be happy?'

'I think so.'

Elizabeth smiled, to dissipate Mrs Grice's slight disapproval of her cynicism. But Mrs Grice was smiling too, reaching into her pocket.

'Fancy me forgetting this! Tom next door brought it over when I had the coffee on just now. It was delivered with their letters by mistake.'

She held it out, a letter from Gwen. Back in the present, Elizabeth was assailed by Sammy's music and turned the knobs until she found something less strident, watching his lowering brow, his crumpling face, as she fiddled. He made a few hopeful gestures to the new programme, then stood still and dejected, his arms hanging.

'Mix me some colours,' suggested Elizabeth, and Sammy grimaced with purpose, trotting over to a corner of the studio where he squatted down in front of a paintbox and some sheets of paper. This was Sammy's equipment, and to mix colours was to paint a picture. Elizabeth always marvelled that Sammy recognised a point where his picture was finished and would never, after that moment, work on it again.

She took the letter.

'I knew you were excited, Gritsy.'

Elizabeth also knew that Gwen was fractionally Mrs Grice's favourite. Was it because we always find most precious that which we're least sure of? Elizabeth felt no jealousy. Gwen was her favourite, too.

'That Police Constable King's a nice young fellow,' said Mrs Grice.

'Um,' said Elizabeth, reading. Gwen hadn't written much. She simply told Elizabeth that she needed her physical presence and the surrounds of home.

'So I'll come on Saturday. Arrive 5.10 I believe, but shan't *expect* you at the station. In fact I'll be annoyed if you change any plans. Love to Sammy and Gritsy. All love to you.'

The note filled the small page, and it was only as she folded it up again that Elizabeth noticed the few words on the back. Gwen had finished up by writing: 'I'm frightened, Elizabeth.'

Elizabeth stuffed letter and envelope into her pinafore pocket. She would have to think, later, about what Gwen had written, but not now, not in front of Gritsy. She smiled and nodded.

'Yes, Gritsy, she's coming. Sammy!' she called, 'Sammy!' He was absorbed, executing great sweeps of blue paint. 'Gwen's coming!'

He looked up, open-mouthed. The heart-breaking suggestion of normal adult emotion began in his eyes. But as always it was lost in a wide simper. Not that he didn't understand her. He placed his brush carefully out of danger and got to his feet. He lumbered over to Elizabeth and put his arms on her shoulders, his cheek against hers.

'Gwen!' he babbled happily, 'Gwen coming. We going to see Gwen, Elibet!'

3

Police Constable Peter King liked a lot of salt with his boiled egg, so it was to an egg without salt that he mentally compared Elizabeth. He felt it was a pity that he should have to do this, because she was so clearly a good egg.

But what is the use of an egg, thought Police Constable King, in conscious parody of 'Alice' because he liked to apply his reading, without piquancy or condiment?

What he meant was, that he couldn't fall in love with her, and couldn't find any real reason why not, she was certainly attractive. Perhaps it was that she wouldn't be able to take anything lightly.

Not that Peter King particularly wanted, himself, to take things lightly, women any more than anything else. But he knew that he could.

Peter King was a policeman by vocation; the inevitability of it filled every corner of his life. He saw his vocation for the Force as a huge illogical fire that had pierced a cool, rational disposition and burned its way through his daily life, its sole but steady source of warmth.

From a working-class family, he had won a scholarship to Cambridge. He hadn't had an ambition then, he had simply been so bright at school that he hadn't been able to avoid being spotted, and nursed in the school's interest, and placed to read Law.

One evening in his final year, still without an idea on his future, he had rounded a quiet corner and found a man struggling with an elderly woman for possession of her handbag. Spurred by instant indignation at injustice, Peter King had run forward and felled the man with an instinctively effective blow to the chin. He then sat on a nearby wall holding the elderly woman's hand until he had restored her. Only then did he telephone the police from a newsagent's shop to report the existence of a senseless thug.

That night, for the first time that he could remember, Peter King had been unable to sleep. It was the impact of a wall of darkness giving way to a long vista with every far detail clear. It had been as simple as that. But the other side of his confidence was a permanent bracing for disaster, like carrying an umbrella on a cloudless day.

He was not impatient for promotion. He knew it would come, and he approved the refusal of the Force to compromise on its serving standards by any special recognition of graduates. He was not bored with Upper Longford: for his assignment as a constable he had asked for a rural area in a County Constabulary rather than a section of a metropolis, fancying a unique role in a microcosmic community. He lodged in quarters for single personnel in neighbouring Great Longford, and when he was off-duty sometimes went back to his parents' house in North London or the house in the next street where his childhood sweetheart had graduated to the role of cheerful local whore.

Peter King came from Great Longford to Upper Longford by bicycle, and rode it over part of his beat. Some of it he chose to walk. His area was wide but the village was small and extremely pretty, the people interesting rather than not, and on foot he could indulge his passion for thoroughness of thought, word and deed.

His colleagues in Great Longford didn't know Peter King very well (nobody did), although they called him the ambitious one. Certainly, he had subdued his London accent on the twin grounds of aesthetics and self-interest...

Peter King saw Elizabeth's fair head move away across the studio as he turned back to admire her house. Peter King considered Melbury Grange, which had been built in the reign of Queen Anne, to be the finest house in Upper Longford, but thought it was rather absurd for Elizabeth to live there alone. In village jargon, Elizabeth was 'big house'. Her parents and grandparents had lived in Melbury Grange, and their parents and grandparents, so she was accorded the village respect due to the house – though not, as she suspected, from Peter King.

Peter King moved on. He was pleased to see Mr Melbury, the vicar, in the churchyard, and hoped for a short tour of eccentric tombstones.

But he didn't reach the vicar. To get from Melbury Grange to the church he had to pass Elizbeth's back gate, and Mrs Grice was in the yard, talking to the birds as she fed them.

The dog Kim tugged eagerly towards her, whimpering, and Peter King slowed down. He was not officially a dog-handler. He had always known that his vocation would stretch happily to include management of a dog, but this would have been to delay his promotion too far. His extraordinary luck – or was he extraordinarily competent? Peter King wasn't sure – had brought him this dog without obligation. It had belonged to a colleague, a man who, despite the dog's gallant support, had died from a bandit's bullet. The dog, who was not young, had gone into a decline, punctuated by periods of snapping attacks on anyone nearby. There was reluctant talk of putting him down. Peter King went to see him, and after the fifth tête-à-tête without violence from Kim, was told he could take the dog on probation.

There was no more trouble. Peter kept Kim with him in Great Longford, and he now allowed gentle approaches from anyone. Peter thought that Kim's salvation was one of the best things he had yet been concerned in.

Mrs Grice favoured Kim, and Kim knew it. He put his front paws on a rung of the gate and waited panting, his feathered tail swinging slowly from side to side.

'Morning, Mr King!'

How nice the policeman looked, wholesome and reassuring! Sometimes Mrs Grice was afraid the world she knew was disappearing, and it was good to see a young person like Police Constable King. Not that he exactly gave an impression of youth, but when you looked in his face you realised he couldn't yet be thirty.

'There's coffee on.' Mrs Grice advanced to fondle the dog. 'And a good plain biscuit for Kim. Won't hurt his figure!'

'Quickly, then.'

But he said it lazily, smiling. He opened the gate and let Kim go, so that the dog led the way through the open kitchen door. Mrs Grice went to a tin and brought out a biscuit, which Kim took gently from her fingers.

Peter sat down at the table. He liked Mrs Grice's kitchen. It reminded him of a kitchen he had known in his extreme youth when his parents had once managed to send him to a farm for a summer holiday, and he had spent nearly all his few indoor hours in the huge kitchen there, permanently inhabited by family and animals.

The kitchen at Melbury Grange held only Mrs Grice and Elizabeth's cat, a large striped animal, rolled up tidily on an armchair and blinking at them, ignoring Kim's brief snuffling investigations. The square wooden table, bleached snow-white with scrubbing, was in the centre of the kitchen, and the enormous range was far enough away for Peter King not to find it oppressive on a warm spring day.

Mrs Grice poured him a mug of coffee and he looked at her with approval.

'Elizabeth misses Gwen,' observed Mrs Grice, making a small pot of dark tea.

'Gwen?'

Mrs Grice looked astonishment at the question in his voice. At the same time she experienced a wave of affection for him at the sight of the band of pressure round his thick straight hair, formed by the helmet he was laying carefully on the table. Any evidence that a clever person, a person she admired, was subject to the laws of nature, touched Mrs Grice.

'You mean you don't know about Gwen?'

'I have to confess it.'

Peter King smiled ruefully, feeling a rogue throb of anticipation.

'Not from Elizabeth, even?'

'I haven't often talked to Elizabeth – Miss Hampson.'

'No, well. Gwen is Elizabeth's sister.'

'Her sister?' He found he was excited.

'Her twin sister.'

Peter King drew in his breath. This news, ridiculously, explained Elizabeth.

He didn't know which question to ask first. He was amazed he had heard nothing from any of his informants in street, pub, and parlour. Mrs Grice spoke again while he was fumbling.

'We hardly ever see Gwen now. She works in London.'

'But surely she has holidays. And Christmas. And Easter.'

'Oh, they don't always mean holidays in *her* job. She's a model.'

Peter King's interest was deflected for a moment on to how Mrs Grice was making this announcement. It was a sort of professional reaction. He thought he could hear both pride and disapproval.

'Oh, yes?' he encouraged politely.

'Quite a well known one. So Elizabeth tells me. I don't know.'

Disapproval, mainly.

'Are they identical?'

He smiled inwardly, but was surprised, at

the tension with which he awaited Mrs Grice's reply.

'Well, yes, they are.'

'You don't sound quite sure! They are or they aren't, you know, Mrs Grice. It's a physical thing.'

'Oh, they are! It was just – to me, you'll understand, they're so different. It sounds absurd to say they're identical, Elizabeth and Gwen! But I know people sometimes haven't been able to tell them apart. Nowadays they're different, though, even to people who don't know them. It's not just their hair...'

Peter King's imagination swung violently about Elizabeth's yellow hair, long, looped up, smooth and shiny. All he knew about Gwen's hair was that it wasn't like that...

'I know what you mean, Mrs Grice. People develop their own personalities whatever the genes say.'

'They did everything the same until they were quite young women. But they never *were* the same, never. Gwen was always the one with the ideas, the ringleader, you might say. If they got into trouble, you could be sure it had begun with Gwen, and she'd talk them out of it...'

There was no mistaking the mood now. Mrs Grice's face shone with tenderness and affection. Gwen must be the favourite.

Mrs Grice had sent herself into a reverie. She went on smiling past him, into the wall.

Peter was wondering what she could see there when a small boy appeared in the kitchen doorway, poking out an envelope. Peter recognised the vicar's youngest son.

'Hello, Tommy.'

'Morning, Mr King, sir.'

Peter King still thrilled to the sound of his name spoken because of his office. It was a sort of endorsement of what he was doing. Now, it slipped a plank under his feet, which had begun to float from the ground.

Tommy thrust from one leg to the other, still extending the envelope. Peter King coughed. Mrs Grice blinked and saw the boy.

'Hello, lad.' She was in front of him, looking down at him. Peter King thought how quickly she moved, for her age and size. 'What have you got there?'

'Letter for Miss Hampson. Came to us by mistake.'

'Thank you, Tommy.'

Mrs Grice glanced at the envelope as she took it, then in conspiratorial delight at Police Constable King. She put the letter on the table beside him and moved across the kitchen. Peter King saw a Chelsea postmark and Elizabeth's name and address in a large and lavish hand.

Mrs Grice took a pastry out of a tin and came back to Tommy.

'I expect you could manage this.'

'Thanks, Mrs Grice.'

Tommy grinned with the pastry already between his teeth, and disappeared. Mrs Grice picked up the letter and sat down at the table. She looked portentously at Peter King.

'Not bad news, I hope?'

'I hope not.' A small shade came and went on her face. 'But – Mr King! It's from Gwen! When we were just talking! She hardly ever writes. Not that Elizabeth writes either. They don't seem to need to. They may be different, but they're very close, you know.'

There was something in the whole quality of the morning that made Peter King feel this development to be inevitable. Indeed, the moment he heard the letter was from Gwen, he had always known it.

'Perhaps she's coming home. If she doesn't write often there must be a reason.'

'Yes…'

Mrs Grice held the letter between her hands. There was a sudden piercing shriek from the kettle. Peter King jumped up in shock, and stayed on his feet. It was a recall to duty.

Mrs Grice got up too.

'I must take them their coffee. Elizabeth works so hard. And Sammy loves his coffee. Mostly milk, you know.'

'Sammy loves Kim.'

'He's the dearest, gentlest soul.'

Peter King looked affectionately at his

dog, then realised Mrs Grice was talking about Sammy.

'What – happened to Sammy?'

'When he was a baby a pillow got on his face. He was found – in time, but the doctor had to give him artificial respiration.'

Mrs Grice spoke matter-of-factly.

'Was he – would he have been normal?'

For a second he saw horror in her face.

'There's no reason to think he wouldn't, Mr King.'

'I suppose the lack of oxygen damaged his brain.'

'Ten seconds would be enough, they said.' Mrs Grice visibly pulled herself together. She poured liquid into mugs. 'At least he's happy. Always happy.'

Peter King picked up Kim's lead, trailing beside him where the dog lay at the foot of the cat's chair. They moved to the door.

'See you, Mrs Grice.'

'Good morning, Mr King. Don't ever go past, will you?'

She always asked him this, and he waited to hear it. It was a sort of option.

4

'Don't pretend to be surprised, darling. You knew I'd come.'

'I hoped you would. But I tend to get surprised, these days, when my hopes are realised.'

This was a disturbing remark, but Great Longford station wasn't the place to comment on it. It delayed for only a second Elizabeth's physical assault on Gwen, which was met half-way and with as much force. The twins hugged each other fiercely, their faces together. Elizabeth smelt a not altogether fragrant scent, too sharp and stirring. Gwen thought of Mrs Grice: Elizabeth had the reassuring aura which had surrounded Mrs Grice when they were children, of cream and newly-ironed warm clothes and fresh flowers.

'Same old car!' said Gwen, sending the boot lid flying.

'I'm afraid so.'

'Oh, darling, I'm not criticising. I'm glad. I want everything to be the same. Everything!'

'It probably is. Want to drive?'

'Oh, no, *no.*'

Gwen flung into the passenger seat. While she waited for Elizabeth her face settled to a sort of repose and Elizabeth, seeing her through the window, was shocked. Gwen looked old, hopeless and defeated. Elizabeth could hardly bear to look at her, or to think about what her appearance might mean. She began to talk as soon as she opened the door.

'It's marvellous that you've come.'

'I had to come.'

Elizabeth remembered the three words on the back of Gwen's letter.

'Had to?'

Gwen burst out laughing, too loud.

'Yes, had to! I suddenly missed you and home and Sammy and Gritsy like instant hell, and I had to come. You know I never deny myself when I *have* to do things!'

'Yes.' Gwen had sometimes had to do things that cut across Elizabeth's inclinations. 'You're lucky to have the sort of job where you can do what you *have* to do.'

Both pairs of eyes slid inwards at the same moment, met briefly, warmly smiled.

'I suppose I am. But I really do work hard Elibet! Harder and harder. So just lately I've been able to call my own halt.'

'You're really quite famous,' said Elizabeth. 'I liked the green and gold do on the front of *Carnival*.'

'You would have done it better. That one.

Too daylight and sunshine for me, really. You would have been perfect.' Gwen glanced at Elizabeth's shining yellow lengths of hair. 'Would I be like that?'

'Like what?'

Gwen touched a strand. 'That?'

'Well – you were, weren't you?'

'Was I? I don't remember. It seems such a long time ago.'

'Why do you take all the colour out of it?' asked Elizabeth, and wished instantly that she hadn't. She knew the answer, anyway, it was because Alan had liked it so much as it was. 'It suits you, though.'

Elizabeth spoke so hard on the heels of her question that she hoped it no longer stood. Certainly Gwen didn't answer it. But Elizabeth wasn't quite happy: if she had really been trying to spare Gwen pain (and need they of all two people ever try to spare each other?), her thin bit of flattery was perhaps justified; but if, as she suspected, her reflex had been one of embarrassment pure and simple, it was ridiculous. There was not enough real stress in her life, to release her from the midgelike bite of nuance. She thought, to her surprise, that's the sort of reason Police Constable King doesn't like me. This time the view as they reached the top of Piper's Slope did nothing for her spirits.

But Gwen said:

'Oh, let's stop here! Let's stop please, Elibet!' and dug firm fingers into her arm.

Elizabeth drew in and stopped. They got out of the car in silence and stood together by a hawthorn hedge, arm in arm. Gwen took a deep breath.

'Just look at it!'

Piper's slope went down snaky and slow between close parallel twists of young green may, turning aside before the dark square of evergreens enclosing the churchyard. The twins looked down on the small fat tower, rosy in the sunshine, and on their own garden with its circles of spring yellow, into one of which Mrs Grice was cutting, making no visible impression.

'Gritsy!' said Gwen and Elizabeth on an instant, and Gwen laughed loud and long.

'For your room, probably,' said Elizabeth, wishing Gwen would stop laughing. 'She's so excited.'

'So am I. You can see that, can't you?'

Gwen thrust her face close to Elizabeth's and opened her eyes very wide, smiling almost savagely. The pupils of her eyes vanished, and although Gwen was facing into a sudden unclouded sun, Elizabeth burst out:

'Darling, I do hope you don't take drugs. Do you?'

It was said. Whatever Gwen's reaction, whatever Elizabeth might have done to the precious days ahead of them, even if she had made them disappear, the question was out and there would be no more painful debate about whether or not to ask it.

Gwen laughed again. 'Oh, darling, I *have* taken drugs. I've done most things.'

'And I've done nothing,' said Elizabeth, her flat tone hiding a sudden stab of pain. 'Soft drugs?' She used the phrase self-consciously.

'Soft drugs. Oh, yes. I have no real urge to self-destruction. And even with the soft stuff – well, it wasn't my answer.'

'What is? What is, Gwen?' Elizabeth was so relieved that she kissed her sister boisterously on the cheek.

'I haven't the faintest idea. I keep stumbling on things that aren't, so by a long process of elimination I should eventually find out.'

Elizabeth's energy and optimism knew no bounds. Mrs Grice, in the garden below, had detached herself from the circle of gold. 'Shall we go home, Gwen?'

'I shouldn't have kept them waiting, but I wanted... Yes, let's go home.'

Before she started the engine Elizabeth turned to Gwen. 'Tell me, darling, please tell me. You said, as if you couldn't help it, you said in your letter: "I'm frightened, Elizabeth". Why did you say that?'

Gwen picked Elizabeth's hand off the steering wheel and held it against her face.

'I'm not frightened now, Elizabeth, not in the least. Doesn't that answer you?'

'Perhaps.'

'I'm not frightened of anything that can have anything done about it. So it was silly of me to say that. It's worried you, I can see it has. For nothing. Let's go home.'

Mrs Grice was not demonstrative. It was Gwen who inaugurated the kissing and hugging. Mrs Grice smiled steadily, even rosier than usual.

'It's been a long time.'

'But when I'm here again, it hasn't been any time at all! I can see myself in the furniture, as usual. All this glowing wood and yellow flowers, I love it.'

'But you put a nice bit of polish on in your flat.'

'Gritsy, you can't polish glass and marble and laminations and plastics. And flowers don't live with the heating. So it's all the more...'

Gwen, who was steadily circling the sitting-room, stopped beside a small shining table. 'This disaster has almost been obliterated by age and elbow-grease. Not in my memory. Do you remember how it happened?'

She was fingering an infinitesimal break in the gleaming surface.

'Yes, Gwen.'

'I don't,' said Elizabeth.

'Temper, darling, pure temper. I *had* to do something – some painting, I think it was (me!), when a walk was scheduled, and I got frustrated.'

'Oh, yes, but there were…'

'…several occasions of the kind? Oh, yes. There were.'

Gwen bounced into an armchair with a laugh and a grimace, but when she was settled back they saw she was crying.

'What is it, darling?'

'Nothing, nothing, Elibet. Reaction. I haven't been home for a long time. You're right, Gritsy, it *has* been a long time.'

Mrs Grice said:

'We miss you very much.' She moved to the door and turned. 'I'll make tea. And Sammy's waiting in the studio. He's painting you a picture.'

'Sammy!' Gwen jumped up. 'I'd forgotten him. Elizabeth, I'd forgotten Sammy!'

Sammy was absorbed in his work, his protruding tongue broke a rapt profile. The sisters tiptoed across the room.

'Sammy,' said Gwen, softly.

He froze in disbelief, then slowly turned his head. Gwen started to run as his arms came out, and they hugged each other a long moment, rocking to and fro. Sammy smacked his lips on Gwen's neck and ear, took her to his picture and guided her hand across its surface, tried to pull her with him on some unintelligible errand. Then he dropped her hand and galumphed over to Elizabeth, to whom he murmured consolatory syllables for his neglect, his arms round her neck.

At last he stood between them, his hands dangling, panting for joy.

'Sit down, for goodness' sake!' said Gwen, when Mrs Grice had deposited the tea tray and was moving towards the door.

'The dinner...'

'To hell with the dinner! I'm sorry, Gritsy, but it doesn't really matter what time we have dinner. Now does it? Tell me, does it matter what time we have dinner?'

Elizabeth wished that Gwen would not go on so much about something so trivial, but Mrs Grice sat down opposite to them and folded her hands.

'Is that better?' she asked.

Gwen laughed rapturously.

'Marvellous. And of course you can go soon, if you must. I'm not selfish enough to want you to stay up beyond your bedtime, because I wouldn't let you get on with the dinner. Well, I probably am. But not just at this moment. All right, darling.'

Gwen gave Sammy, who was nudging her and pointing to the tray, a plate with a large piece of cake. She placed the mug of milk in front of him. 'Are you all as well as you look?'

'I don't know. How do we look?'

'*You* look all right, Elizabeth,' said Mrs Grice. Her eyes lingered approvingly on Elizabeth's face. The bones were not quite so pronounced as Gwen's and the skin glowed a rosy brown. 'You don't look so well, Gwen.'

'Don't I, Gritsy?'

Elizabeth sensed a warning, but Mrs Grice was prepared to repeat her charge, without confusion.

'No, you don't, Gwen, and that's a fact.'

'Too thin, or what?'

'No, I can't exactly say that. Too – pale perhaps, too sharp in the face. As if you were getting over an illness.'

'Oh, if I only was!'

Elizabeth noted another disturbing remark. Mrs Grice got up and went out with the tray.

'It's drinks time, really,' said Gwen, looking at her watch. 'Only I'm too full of tea.'

'There's stuff there.'

'I'm sure. Later.'

The sisters sat in silence to Sammy's bubbling obbligato, while the garden faded with the light. Elizabeth thought of the series of dusks before her which Gwen would share. Her uneasiness ... it was just that feeling of uncertainty which always assailed her the first hours they were reunited.

'Tell me about you, Elibet,' said Gwen at last, and Sammy stopped babbling to gaze open-mouthed into her face. 'Not a word yet. Not that I've given you a chance.'

They heard footsteps overhead. Gwen half rose, then checked herself.

'What's the matter, darling?'

'You know what she's doing?'

'Gritsy?'

'She's unpacking for me. She shouldn't!'

'Don't try to stop her. Oh, don't!'

Gwen sank back. 'Of course not. And I haven't brought...'

Elizabeth saw half a moon, thin as lace. It was in a sky made midnight blue by the table light glowing beside the sofa.

'You, Elibet?'

'I enjoy life,' said Elizabeth, surprised that she spoke so firmly. Was she expecting to be contradicted?

'That – is – clear. Oh, Elibet, the times I lie in bed, and wonder why it hasn't been given me to be as happy as my sister!'

'Gwen!'

'Oh, don't try to make anything *significant* out of it. It's merely our temperaments. If it wasn't – well, I could live at Melbury Grange too, perhaps. As it is, my love affair with Melbury Grange must consist of a series of ravishing reunions which wouldn't survive daily life.'

'A well-spaced series.'

Gwen took Elizabeth's hand.

'Do you wish I came home more often?'

'Of course I do. But only if you wanted to.'

'I do, I think.' Gwen released the hand with a pressure. 'But what have you been *doing*, darling, who have you been *seeing?*'

'I've been working. You know how lucky I am that way, it's play as well.'

'Working on anything special?'

'Oh, not really. Just the usual round of commissions. And the odd thing to please myself.'

Elizabeth hadn't known whether or not she wanted Gwen to see her own portrait, because of the way it was turning out. As she spoke she decided she would keep it hidden for the length of Gwen's stay.

'Making much money?'

'Making more.'

'So we don't have to worry so much as we did about keeping the Grange going?'

'We still would, without your help. And the Trust money. As it is, I manage. The funny thing is, though…'

Elizabeth stopped.

'What's the funny thing? No, I don't really have to ask you. You're not so sure as you were that you want to keep it going?'

'Something like that, yes. Oh, I don't want to leave Upper Longford, I belong here. But sometimes I feel a bit – inappropriate – in this huge house.' She had first defined the sensation after a conversation in the lane with Police Constable King. 'Sometimes I think – perhaps one of those cottages below the vicarage. With the Grange being listed I wouldn't be abandoning it to destruction. And it might be made *useful*. I've sometimes thought…'

'What?'

'That children like Sammy might go to school here.'

'You're not such a stick-in-the-mud as I sometimes think you are,' said Gwen. 'Me, now, I shudder with horror at the thought of no longer belonging at Melbury Grange. And I don't even live here.'

'It's because you're not used to the idea. One can get used to the idea of things.'

'Oh, one can, darling, one can!'

Elizabeth went over to the window. The moon now rode with the clouds in a burnished ring, so bright that when she looked down to the gate she didn't at first see the bobbing circle of torchlight. But as her eyes cleared of moon dazzle she noticed a dark shape beyond the light point and identified it by the unique structure of its summit.

'Darling!' Gwen stood up at the liveliness of Elizabeth's voice. 'If it isn't our friendly neighbourhood policeman! Exercising his dog in our very lane. Let's go out and meet him!' She turned from the window. 'Come on! Before he disappears.'

'All right, dear. But is he special, or something?'

'Not really,' said Elizabeth, checked so that it was Gwen who led the way to the door. 'It's just that he's – I think he's the only person I've "seen" since you were last home! And there's something about him.' She revived. 'Come and see! But I think what I really want is to show you off.'

They found a mac and an anorak in the cloakroom. Elizabeth wondered what she really did want. It could be, to show Police Constable King another dimension of herself, by showing him her sister.

The air was sharp, tapping their cheeks with memories of winter, but so softly that it promised the summer to come. Gravel scrunched as they went down the path, and Kim's pointed ears broke the line of hills far away. He had put his front paws on a rung of the gate.

'Good evening, Mr King,' said Elizabeth primly, no longer having to show liberal balance in her own person.

'Hello, there – Miss Hampson?'

Police Constable King shone his torch gradually upwards towards Elizabeth's voice. Its beam was powerful, and spilled over on to Gwen, beside her.

The three stood in silence, Elizabeth triumphant, Gwen mildly interrogative, Police Constable King absorbing the fact of the two women so that for a few seconds he had no thoughts at all.

Afterwards he could not remember another time when the evidence of his eyes had been so overwhelming as utterly to preclude thought. It is rare that our anticipations, which tend towards the ideal, are fully realised. But when thought came back to Peter King, he knew that a perfect version of Elizabeth was waiting beside her. It was like being permitted to glance from the flawed human reality to the Platonic ideal. The impact was so strong that he felt faint and had to reach for the support of the gate.

Elizabeth broke the silence.

'Witchcraft, Mr King!'

'It could be.' He spoke very quietly, as if there was indeed a breakable spell.'

'But you knew. I must have spoken to you about my sister Gwen.'

'Mrs Grice did. Good evening – Miss Hampson.'

Now he felt and sounded like a policeman.

'Good evening, Mr – King, did Elizabeth say?'

'Peter King. Isn't it a wonderful night?'

'It's perfect,' said Gwen. 'I can hear the silence. Listen a moment!'

Elizabeth heard murmurs from the neighbouring hedges, the surrounding fields. Peter King's head just then was full of sound rather like bells, but from his solitary night walks he knew what she meant, he had heard the components of country silence.

'There are so many tiny sounds that make up silence,' said Gwen. 'It's ridiculous to say that silence is *silent.* Only death would be that.'

They stood without speaking, then, their faces raised and angled as if to catch the offerings of the night. An owl hooted softly; some small animal gave a brief shriek of fear or pain. Peter King regretted he had no quotation available in which to encapsulate the moment, and his state of heart. To his annoyance he heard himself ask:

'Are you staying long, Miss Hampson?'

'I presume you're speaking to me,' said Gwen, 'and I don't know how long I'm staying.'

'As long as I can keep her,' said Elizabeth. 'It must have been awkward with twins in the days when "Miss Smith" persisted even into close friendship. I mean, if I was older than Gwen I'd be Miss Hampson, and she'd be Miss Gwendolen. Quite simple. What did twins do?'

'Not even twins are born simultaneously,' said Gwen, 'which means that in our case *I* am Miss Hampson and you Miss Elizabeth.'

Peter King was saying 'Gwen' in his mind, over and over again. He could hardly wait to pronounce the syllable aloud. Gwen's remark made this impossible, even in humorous quotes.

'Good night, Miss Hampson. Good night,

Miss Elizabeth.'

They each caressed Kim through the bars. Peter King's eager torch shone on four identical hands.

'Yes,' said Gwen, as she took off Elizabeth's anorak in the hall. 'Quite the best-looking young man I've seen.' She looked hard at Elizabeth, whose honesty and modesty made her recoil. Before she had thought she said:

'Oh, not for *me!*'

Peter King went slowly back to the village, to off-duty and his supper date with one of the fruitiest of the local characters. He wondered if he had reached a watershed, or if there was as yet enough evidence to know. It could as well be spring fever, or the reaction of unconscious boredom.

He didn't even know whether he had gone by chance that night into Melbury Lane, or with purpose and hope.

5

For dinner Mrs Grice served everything Gwen had once liked best. There was even syrup sponge. Without accepting a second helping Gwen was enthusiastic and remarked on each evidence of Mrs Grice's memory and indulgence.

'You probably need some good feeding up.'

'Gritsy,' explained Gwen, with perfect good humour, 'if I were to feed up I would lose my job. It's like being a jockey.'

Mrs Grice sniffed. 'I know. I see the magazines. How many normal women look like that – long drinks of water and faces all eyes!'

'Me, Gritsy?'

'Well, no, pet, though you could do with some colour. But – you're so different from the most of us. How can *you* sell the clothes?'

'Ah, Gritsy, there's always the lurking hope that the clothes will make the figure, that if you buy the dress, you'll buy how *I* look in it. And so they fall. Because the dress I'm wearing *doesn't* look like them.'

'They're exploited.'

'Of course they are. Aren't we all? All the

time, one way or another. And if we resist here, we fall there, we're got at from every side. It's one of the nastier aspects of consumer society.'

'Why do you do it, Gwen?'

It was impossible to tell, from Mrs Grice's good-natured, placid face, if this was curiosity or sorrow.

'I do it because I was found to have the qualifications, and I can do it well, and it earns good money. The best reasons for doing a job. And as it won't pay all that long, I'll do it while I can. It's honest.' Mrs Grice looked down at her plate. 'Oh, if there was a spontaneous renunciation of the consumer society I'd no doubt join it, and take deep gulps of fresh air. But not unless and until. Any more than Elizabeth would give up the car all on her own because of pollution. Gritsy, I'm all right. Truly, dearest.'

Mrs Grice looked up at Gwen, smiling. 'You should be, you're a Hampson.'

Elizabeth was finding her spirits alarmingly acrobatic. Now, from the trough into which they had fallen since the encounter she had manoeuvred with Police Constable King, they bounded up again.

'Let's have coffee by the studio fire.'

Mrs Grice got up. 'You two.'

'We're all washing up,' said Elizabeth firmly. 'At least, I am.'

'I'll help you. First, though – will Sammy

be asleep?'

'Maybe not. Go and see.'

In the end they had coffee at the kitchen table, listening to Mrs Grice recalling incidents of their childhood, adding details and anecdotes of their own. Seeing the back staircase disappearing upwards in the corner, Elizabeth remembered, with a reminiscent shiver, how it had once terrified her. But Gwen remembered more of the past than Elizabeth did – more detail, more small events.

'Perhaps it isn't strange, really, Elibet. You see, you haven't had to remember, you've gone on having it. I had to break it off, so I wrapped it up and put it away.'

Mrs Grice was moved by the extent of Gwen's memory. She said once:

'Oh, Gwen, I would never have thought you'd remember *that!*'

'Gritsy, you'd be surprised. I think of you some time during every single day.'

'Are you happy?'

'I don't think about being happy, or not. But I *was* happy then, that's for sure. Because it's gone and been sealed off and nothing can touch it.'

'You weren't always happy then,' said Elizabeth.

'Good God, Elizabeth!' Gwen was pink for once, with annoyance. Tears of anger shone in her eyes. 'I'm not such an idiot as to imagine I was, *at the time.* I'm happy in it now, the past. That's all that counts. It didn't end in a bang, it's safe. Don't you see?'

'Yes. Yes, I do.'

She did, of course, but had never, in her own life, made any change drastic enough to do anything more to the past than let it fade away pleasantly behind her.

Gwen's rage went as suddenly as it had come. She put a hand out to each of them, laughing.

'I'm not unhappy all the time, Gritsy, I promise you.'

'The fire will want attention,' said Mrs Grice. 'Go and see to it and have a talk. Do you know how late it is? I'm going to bed when I've got myself ready for the morning.'

'Shall we say good night, then?'

'Yes. Good night, pet. Sleep well. No dreams.'

Gwen put her arms round Mrs Grice. 'You always used to say that, and I never thought it was much of a wish. I *liked* dreaming.'

'But you had nightmares.'

'I had sweet dreams more often.'

'Sweet dreams, then.'

Mrs Grice held Gwen's face for a minute between her hands and looked at it. She and Elizabeth laid their faces together, as always.

'Gritsy's getting old,' said Elizabeth in the studio. She put a large new log across the thin glowing strips of wood. It crackled instantly, sending a flare of golden sparks into the velvet darkness of the cowl.

'That's a very old remark,' said Gwen, as Elizabeth settled back beside her. 'I mean, it's the sort of remark old people make. All I can do with it is to accord it a two minute silence. Elibet, what are you doing with yourself apart from working?'

'Thinking. Walking. Reading. Listening to music. Encouraging Sammy.'

'Exactly. You're not having contact.'

'I see the W.I. people fairly regularly.'

'Oh, I suppose you do! But – aren't there any men around?'

'None that interest me.'

'You seem to be interested in the local police constable.'

'Oh, Gwen! No, I'm not really. It's just that – well, he does seem to be the only faintly interesting man around, if one thinks about it. Just as well I'm so self-sufficient.'

'Not so well at all. If you weren't you'd *do* something and it would be good for you.' Gwen exhaled smoke, which drifted in a ring towards the fire. 'Don't pull that silly face, Elibet. There are lots of things a girl can do without making herself ridiculous – or unladylike, if that matters, which I think with you it does.'

'If she can be bothered.'

'She must be bothered. And it puzzles me

that you can do such good work.'

'Not that old argument! What about Emily Brontë?'

'She was a genius.'

'Touchée.'

'I didn't mean…'

'Yes, you did, and quite right. And I suppose experience does help creativity. But I can't feel my dust jackets are suffering because I don't go to bed in company.'

'Never?'

'Never.'

Elizabeth looked steadily at Gwen, who started to laugh again. The laughter went on and on, punctuated by coughing as Gwen choked on smoke. Elizabeth struggled between irritation and concern.

'What's so funny?' she had to ask at last. Gwen wiped her eyes and lit another cigarette.

'Forgive me, darling. It was just – thinking that we each have the same preoccupation about each other – from opposite ends. You – because I do. I – because you don't. Oh, there's no happy mean in this world.'

'We form one between us?' suggested Elizabeth.

'Oh, Elibet!'

Gwen put her arms round Elizabeth.

'It even explains,' said Elizabeth, 'why I rushed us out to Police Constable King. I wanted to show him my other self.'

'Elibet!'

'Don't cry any more. We're so lucky.'

'But I neglect you so.'

'You'll come if I need you.'

'And vice versa. Come and stay with me in London soon, Elibet. I'll rout out my least hectic friends.'

'I'd like it.'

'I'll find someone for you to love.'

'Oh, God, Gwen!'

Elizabeth jumped to her feet in annoyance, stumped across the room and pulled the curtains over, against the full moon.

Gwen got up too, and came to stand beside her.

'Don't be cross, darling. Most of us need a prop for most of the time. We can't support ourselves.' Gwen put her hands on Elizabeth's shoulders and kissed her. 'What time do you go to bed alone?'

'About eleven, I suppose.'

'You really do have a bedtime!' Gwen looked at her watch. 'It's eleven now. Unbelievable but it is. Tonight at least, darling, go to bed at your usual time. I'm suddenly terribly tired. But I'd like to dream down here for a while.'

'Of course!'

Elizabeth respected and admired a need for solitude, even between herself and Gwen. 'I'll bring you breakfast in bed tomorrow. It's easier anyway.'

'I'd love it. The first morning, at least. But no great Gritsy do. Thin toast and coffee.'

'I know.' Elizabeth added a log. 'I'm going to look at Sammy now. Good night, darling. All night through my sleep I'll know you're here.'

'All night, through my sleep or not as the case may be, I'll know that I am.'

They kissed. Elizabeth turned round in the doorway and saw Gwen sink back on the sofa, stretching her legs out to the fire.

Presently Gwen heard Elizabeth overhead, and knew she would be turning her, Gwen's, bed down, putting the electric blanket on, seeing that the right complement of Melbury Grange towels, soap, face-cloths, was at her service. Gwen realised that she had never entertained a visitor overnight, unless it was a man in her own bed, had never laid out towels and a breakfast tray. It sounded an innocently happy occupation.

But she was worried about Elizabeth.

Gwen got up, went to the french window, unlocked and opened it. The silence seemed profound, but a few seconds' listening revealed its myriad layers of tiny noises – animal, vegetable, occasionally mineral as a car revved below in the clear air.

Elizabeth should have someone of her own. Someone she could hardly wait to tell things to, someone who could hardly wait to be told, someone who made life – Simone de Beauvoir had said it – a rainbow-coloured short-cut to happiness. Someone – *dear God! – the someone I need. Oh help me, help me! I've brought myself with me, after all.*

Gwen shut the french window and ran blindly back to the sofa. She sat upright on the edge of it, holding herself tight.

God, dear God, if I can just hold on.

Her whirling thoughts had a glimpse of Police Constable King, and were slightly steadied. A black shape with a torch, in the dark. Someone of whom Elizabeth had said: 'He's got something.' For Elizabeth? 'Oh, no, darling, not me!' For Gwen? *I can't wait and see about things, any longer. It's too late. It's too fast. 'I am the light of the world.' Slow down. I can't slow down. With help could I slow down?*

A door opened, and Gwen swung round.

'Hello!' she said. And smiled.

Police Constable King moved through his evening as if it was a pleasant dream.

In a way he rather specially enjoyed himself, because he wasn't as cerebral as usual over what he was doing, and simply absorbed the food and drink and hospitality and the cheerful surroundings, finding them good.

Old Ted Harkness had gone to quite a bit of trouble to entertain him. He'd dragged out his big oak table and put the leaves up. He'd got quantities of cider from the Wheatsheaf, as well as four of their oval pies. He'd even bought rabbit food, as he called it, and opened a jar of his niece's sweet pickled walnuts. To follow the pies was a great hunk of crumbling Cheshire cheese with the niece's onions standing by, and fresh bread and butter.

'Not bad, Mr Harkness,' said Peter at the end of things, frantically overfull, submerging a burp, automatically moderating his praise to the rural understatement which represented the decent local heights of approbation. 'You're a fair host.'

'Thank you, Mr King. It's not often as I have a visitor, these days.'

Ted Harkness poured more cider, talking about his neighbours and then, increasingly, about the past.

'I shall never have had a past,' said Peter King, sighing. He felt mellow and sentimental, and forgot that he was more interested in a collective past than his personal one, in the characteristics shared by wartime working-class childhoods than his own unremarkable recollections. Perhaps if he'd lived in a village, like Ted Harkness... The inanimate in Ted's life had been as gnarled as the human. It made for memories.

When he left Ted, Peter King need have had nothing to do but go home. He was not on duty until the morning. But he decided to take a last check, give Kim a last run.

In his comfortable slacks and sweater, soft-shoed, he made his way towards the upper village and Melbury Lane.

Almost at once the few street lights were left behind. The scattered houses were dark, except for one cottage where the fanlight was illumined by a weak glow. Peter King would have been alarmed if he had not seen this tiny beacon. Alice Harper always slept with her passage light on.

He was a little out of breath when he reached the Grange – from over-eating and a queer sort of apprehension rather than the gradual slope. He laid his arms on the top bar of the front gate, feeling the light frost on his face and feet. He looked at the dark house. There was a warmer light than the moon spilling on to the lawn one side, perhaps through the french window of the studio. He couldn't be sure because the thick curtains of the other studio window, the one that faced him were close drawn.

There was no light anywhere else. Smoke curled very slowly from a high chimney, darker than the moonlit sky.

One moment there was peace, layered in depths of quiet and murmurings, and the next the night was torn open in a series of dreadful raucous human screams. Peal after peal rang out, as if to assure Peter King he had not imagined the horror of the one before. They were screams of terror, disbelief, possibly pain. They came unmistakably from the house in front of him.

The screams were succeeded by silence as dramatic and total. There was no echo except in his mind, where he thought the screams would ring for ever. Even as he wrenched the gate open he heard beyond Kim's whimpering the restored screech of a rodent and the puffy sighing of a dove.

Peter King tore across the grass, round the angle of the house to where the pale line stretched from the french window. As he reached it he saw that one point of light shone low down inside. Expecting resistance he turned the door handle so sharply that the door flew inwards and he almost fell into the room.

Simultaneous with his crashing entry, Elizabeth erupted through the door from the hall. She wore a long dressing-gown and her hair was all over her face. Peter saw her push it back with one hand, looking at him briefly and without surprise, and then they both turned towards the fire, which still glowed. Sammy was standing in front of it, outlined by the red logs, brandishing a sort of small sword, growling and snarling like an animal, his face a mixture of terror and threat.

As his feet lay Gwen, on her back, her head to one side facing Peter King, her eyes looking steadily ahead, her mouth half smiling. Her arms were outspread, one leg was bent, one shoe off.

When he saw Elizabeth Sammy's growling turned into a sobbing whimper and he ran towards her, throwing away the sword. Elizabeth opened her arms.

Police Constable King heard himself call out 'Be careful!' Elizabeth shot him an unbelieving stare. He saw that Mrs Grice had come into the room behind Elizabeth, and was looking dazedly from Sammy to Gwen.

When he had almost reached Elizabeth Sammy stopped, arched his back and threw his arms in the air. He stood like that, straining upwards and back, for what seemed to Peter King like minutes, then collapsed. He fell full length, in one heavy movement, his arms ahead of him, so that his fingers slid down the back of the sofa as if he was clutching for a hold.

He was dead, though. Police Constable King thought so, and knew it as soon as he turned Sammy over and saw the lolling tongue and staring eyes.

Mrs Grice fell on her knees beside Peter King, feeling blindly for Sammy's head, embracing it. She looked up at Elizabeth fiercely as Elizabeth stood frozen between the two bodies.

'He was so happy! Elizabeth, he was so happy and harmless!' Mrs Grice slipped her angry gaze on and off Peter King. 'He never hurt anybody. He was so happy!'

Elizabeth stumbled towards Gwen, and Peter King swivelled round and crossed the carpet on his knees to be there first. He took her wrists as her hands strayed over Gwen's body.

'Mustn't touch.' He put an arm round her shoulder and set her gently aside, leaning her against the front of the sofa where she stayed, staring into space. He thought for the only time that her eyes were like Gwen's. He turned back to Gwen and put his head on her breast. There was no sound. He took her wrist in his fingers and there was no pulse. Then he noticed a thin red line on her light dress, just above the waist, and a fleck of blood in the corner of her mouth.

He bent near to her to close her eyes, then recollected he was a policeman, and left them open. He merely removed a tear from her cheek, because it was his own.

He smelt perfume on her, not death, but she was dead. He remained on his knees.

Elizabeth made a strangled sound in her throat, and with a supreme effort Peter King sat back on his heels and turned to her. They helped each other to their feet. Mrs Grice was still beside Sammy, stroking his mottled forehead.

Peter King looked at his watch.

'Where's the telephone?'

'There's one in the hall.' Elizabeth saw

Kim, sitting still but alert in a corner. She said: 'He's a good dog.'

'Yes, he is.' He took her hand. 'Come along.' They moved slowly over to Mrs Grice, and Peter King squeezed Elizabeth's hand and let it go. He took Mrs Grice gently but firmly under the arms and got her up. She offered no resistance, beyond the resistance of her collapsed weight. When she was on her feet she turned round and looked at Gwen, her face ugly with love and suffering.

'Gwen?' she said, looking up at Elizabeth as if asking a question.

'Gwen's dead,' said Elizabeth, and Mrs Grice stood still, her face turned away from them. Police Constable King saw that her hands were clenching and unclenching at her sides.

'Come along,' said Elizabeth, in her turn, looking at Peter King. He nodded, and she led Mrs Grice out of the room.

Peter King went across to the french window, took out a handkerchief, and used it to lock the doors. After a short search he found what Sammy had thrown away and stood looking down at it. It was a small ornamental sword.

Then with the briefest of downward glances he skirted the two dead and left them together, locking the studio door behind him.

6

Peter King came back at noon next day to Melbury Grange, when he was sure the Detective Chief Superintendent for whom he'd telephoned would have left, and his Detective Inspector, and the paraphernalia of police photographers and fingerprint and footprint experts, and Gwen and Sammy.

He came to the front gate, and saw Elizabeth through the studio window, standing motionless in the middle of the room. She was turned away from him, but he could see that her head was back, her body tensed.

Peter King moved away, towards the back of the house. Elizabeth didn't hear him. She was looking at the two chalk marks on the floor of the studio and trying to take in that they were all that was left of Gwen and Sammy. If she could swallow on this fact, accept the horror of it, it might become easier to bear.

No one should have to bear this.

But I do. It has happened.

Moments of panic came to disturb the steady immovable weight of her loss. They were waves of pain she had to brace herself to withstand. They came when the relentless procession of quotations and pictures across her mind flared too vividly. How could she be expected to live through the next moment, then the next and the next, and know that there were years of moments ahead? What could she do?

There was nothing to do but go to Gritsy. They would help each other because they were each as forlorn.

But the back door bell rang, and Mrs Grice would be occupied. If it was another policeman, he would come and find her. Draggingly, forcing a last look at the diagram that defaced the studio floor, Elizabeth came out and locked the door. She went into the sitting-room, because she must go somewhere, turned on the fire, and huddled in the hearth beside it.

When Mrs Grice answered his ring Police Constable King thought the red-brown of her face had changed. Now it was just a layer of small veins over pallor. Her brown eyes looked deeper, smaller, but lit up when she saw him.

He took her hand and held it for a moment.

'Why isn't she lying down?'

'She should be.' Mrs Grice shut the door behind him. Yesterday she would have left it open. Peter King agreed that now it should be shut. He realised at that moment that to draw the curtains on a death in the house was an instinct before it was a custom.

'So should you. Have you slept?'

'No. I don't imagine you have either, Mr King.'

'Well…'

He had walked. Off the case an hour after reporting it, having made his statement, he had walked before finding his bicycle, and again when he had reached his digs. There had been time left only to douse his head in the basin and put on his uniform.

'May I have some coffee?'

'Oh, gladly!'

The water was ready. When she had given him a mug of coffee Mrs Grice made tea and sat down at the table at right angles, near enough for him to put his hand out and cover her plump pink one, stilling its play with a teaspoon.

They looked at one another, each image blurred by tear-filled eyes.

'Why are you crying, Mr King?'

'Because of you and – Elizabeth.'

It was. He couldn't cry for himself and Gwen.

'You're a good boy.' She patted his hand as she removed her own from beneath it. 'Mr King, it wasn't Sammy! They'll say it was, but it wasn't. It couldn't have been!'

'Why not, Mrs Grice?'

'He had no harm in him. None. He couldn't have hurt a fly. He was always happy. He was excited at seeing Gwen. Whenever Gwen came home Sammy … Sammy…'

She choked, shaking her head. One grey-brown strand of hair was detached from the neat surround and hung over her face. She pushed it away and it trailed untidily down.

'What did they do? Have they talked to you?'

'Oh, yes, they took statements. But what could we state, Elizabeth and I?'

'What was – the weapon?'

'Oh, it's a little sword that Gwen brought back once from a trip to Spain. We kept it on a table by the window with some other knick-knacks.'

'Did they – look round?'

'Everywhere, I should say. In our rooms as well.'

'They always do.'

'I suppose they must.'

'I'm sorry.'

'But we were glad! About that, I mean. We thought: they can't be certain about Sammy.'

'The police are never certain, Mrs Grice, of anything which they don't see. Why did you come downstairs last night?'

She lowered her head over her teacup, and he had a glimpse of a tired old woman.

'Forgive me, you've had enough questions and no real rest. And I've no excuse. I'm not on the case. Uniformed men never are.'

'I know. Elizabeth asked them if you would be.'

The cat jumped down from its chair, crossed the kitchen on tiptoe, and leaped on to Mrs Grice's knees. There wasn't much room between her bosom and the table, and a few silent seconds went by before its head erupted in triumph over the edge, blinking at Peter King. Mrs Grice stroked it, expertly and absently.

'Where's Kim?'

'I left him at home.'

'I came down because I heard the screams – dreadful…' She shuddered, and the cat preened under the movement.

Why was he asking these questions, anyway? It was all being taken care of. But something had struck him.

'Whose screams were they?'

He was aware of the angry clacking of a blackbird beyond the window and the steady tick of a clock. He waited.

'Poor Sammy. His screams killed him. Perhaps he found…'

'What, Mrs Grice?'

'The french window was unlocked, Mr King.'

Her tears suddenly spilled over.

'Mrs Grice, forgive me. Isn't there someone who could come and cope in the house for a day or two, while you rest up a bit?'

She got to her feet.

'You'll be wanting to see Elizabeth. No, Mr King, thank you. I'll lie down this afternoon. Yes, I promise you. And for the rest of it – I'd rather be busy. We both would.'

'Miss Hampson – is working?'

'She will be tomorrow.'

'Might I see her, then? Will you ask her, at least? I shan't expect...'

He even sat down again, in case, but Mrs Grice said:

'Come along, Mr King.'

He followed her to the sitting-room. He hung back in the hall while quiet words were exchanged. Mrs Grice came out to him.

'She wants to see you.'

She closed the door on him. Elizabeth was sitting forward in an armchair, her hands hanging between her knees. He could imagine it a characteristic pose, particularly if she was assessing her work, but now each limb had a languor, a weight to it. When she heard him she moved only her head. Her mouth didn't relax from its imposed control, but he thought there was welcome, even relief, in her eyes.

Peter King went and sat on the arm of her chair, putting his hand on her shoulder. He thought it would be easier if they didn't look at one another. He was aware of a reflex small nestling movement she made briefly against him. Like an animal burrowing for safety. He said:

'I am concerned for you.'

'Thank you.'

She was rigid again. His cheek felt the knot of her hair. He wanted to tell her that he ached, too, but it would be an outrage.

'I'm not on the case, as you know.'

'No,' she said absently, but he went on.

'The C.I.D. investigate crimes. The uniforms prevent it. I'm sorry. I wasn't in time.'

Elizabeth burst out passionately, throwing his hand off as she shook her head:

'It wasn't Sammy! It couldn't have been Sammy, however it looked! He loved us both. Both the same. We were his life. If Sammy killed Gwen – I don't know anything about anything, any more. I'm lost.'

He caught her chin in his hand as she went on fiercely shaking her head, and held it while he turned her face up towards him. He tried to look at it objectively, fairly to assess the quality of its conviction.

'You really mean that?'

'Oh, God, can't you see I mean it? I *know.* I'll never believe Sammy did it, never, whatever they say, however it looked...'

He had never yet seen Elizabeth moved beyond self-consciousness. He wondered if this was the first time. She was so like Gwen now he had to stay silent a moment, for the spasm to pass. While he waited he noticed that, like Mrs Grice, Elizabeth's health was today only skin deep. But her frantic eyes were white-rimmed. She hadn't wept.

'Didn't they give you a sedative?'

'They wanted to. Their doctor looked at me.'

'You should have taken it.'

'Should I? And the waking up?' Her face was dreadful. He had to look away. She said at last:

'I know I saw him with the stiletto. I know I saw his face as I've never seen it before. Angry. But none of that could mean…'

'You've never seen Sammy angry before?'

'Never.'

'You must tell them. Did you tell them?'

'Of course I did. I told them he must have been angry at – what had been done to Gwen. They've examined the french window and the path, you know! The french window was unlocked. It never was unlocked, by that time of night.'

'I know it was unlocked. I came in that way.'

He thought again about those moments after the screams. Remembered the stubbornness of the gate in the dark and his fumbling fingers. His eyes had been on the gate, probing futilely, his ears were full of the echo of obscene noises. It had taken time. Precious seconds. He had seen and heard nobody but…

'Kim whimpered. I thought it was the screams. It seemed to take ages, unlatching the gate. Somebody could have run out through the french window. If they'd taken any route but the front gate I probably shouldn't have known.'

'The police must think it's possible.'

'Don't put too much on that. What the police must do, is look into every remotest possibility. They can't take for granted anything that they don't see.'

'The remotest possibility is that Sammy – it's disgusting.'

She got to her feet and flung about the room. Peter King watched her. She stopped by a small shining table and fingered a blemish on its surface. She said, looking down at the table:

'Do you remember, years ago – last night – she said: "It's mad to say that silence is silent. Only death could be that."'

'I remember.'

Elizabeth raised her arms and clapped her hands to her head. 'The silence is roaring in my ears!'

She dashed herself down on the sofa and burst into passionate crying. Peter King was relieved to see it. As the sobbing diminished he went to sit beside her, not touching her, waiting until she raised her face and felt for a handkerchief. She blew her nose, and he leaned back with her inside his arm.

'It's good to cry,' he said. If he could only do the same, in the quiet of his room!

'Remember I'm here. I'll be here all the time, even if I'm not actually sitting beside you.'

She didn't respond. Peter King let the silence go on, occasionally stroking her hair. In the end, he had never touched Gwen's hair, never once touched it. He doubled up briefly with pain. At last he said, conversationally and to help them both:

'It might have been me, you know.'

He felt her stiffen, distracted.

'How? You?'

'Well, it could have been. What did you see when you opened the studio door?'

'I saw...'

'Apart from... What was I doing?'

'Coming in. Sort of falling in.'

'I might have been going out.'

She considered.

'Making it look... I suppose you might.' The suggestion of a smile came and went. 'Were you?'

'No. But I'm trying to show you what the police have to contend with in a crime nobody saw committed.'

'Did they grill you?'

'Yes. And of course, I couldn't really set their minds at rest, because nobody had seen *me*. I'd taken rather a long time to stroll up from the village, simply because I was overfed. How does that sound?'

'Very thin. And why were you strolling up, anyway?'

'I wanted to make a last check, a last walk for Kim, and ... the church, the vicarage, Melbury Grange – gave me a small goal.'

She looked at him curiously, then he saw the distraction lose its grip, like a physical thing which released her face. It grew bleak and expressionless.

'But they'll come back to Sammy.'

'They possibly will.'

'Oh, God, it wasn't him, whatever they'll say! However it seems. That's why he was angry! And frightened.' She gave a residual violent sob. 'Poor terrified darling.'

'There *is* something wrong somewhere,' admitted Police Constable King. Elizabeth turned to him sharply. Their faces were only a few inches apart. Strain made her more and more like Gwen and for another moment he couldn't speak for his own pain.

'What!'

'I don't know – what. But something... I felt it last night.'

He didn't know what. He only knew that when he had seen Gwen's peaceful face, behind his own anguish something had started to puzzle the policeman. But remembering her face now he said gently to Elizabeth:

'You saw, didn't you, that your sister didn't die in fear – or revolt ... she couldn't have looked like that...'

Elizabeth's eyes filled up again and spilled slowly over. It was like spring rain after winter storms. Peter King waited. She said at last, quietly, and simply as a statement:

'There isn't anyone left, you know.'

'I know. I know, Elizabeth.' To give her her name, without having been invited to, was all he had to give her. He hoped it might be something. He forced himself to smile at her. 'You have me, actually. My spare time is yours, if you want it. To talk to. To try and understand.'

She gave him a swift, surprised glance. 'Yes. You do understand. I've realised. You're – an unusual man, Mr King.'

'My name is Peter.' She smiled faintly, politely. He thought it was a good sign.

'I'm keeping you – Peter. You're on duty.'

'I'll go just now. Why did you come downstairs last night?'

She was surprised.

'Because of the dreadful screams. Terrible.'

'Whose screams were they?'

'Why – I – Sammy's, of course.'

'But you didn't think "Sammy!" before you got into the studio and saw…?'

'No. No, I didn't. I thought … oh, just a wicked awful sound. I only thought – to get downstairs and find out.'

'Yes, of course.' He felt the puzzle should have been clearer. But it wasn't.

'How long – how long had Gwen been – dead?'

‘Not more than half an hour before they all got here. It doesn’t help.’

‘The police were everywhere. But they don’t tell you what they think.’

‘They don’t know themselves, yet.’

‘Oh, they think it’s Sammy. So do you. Don’t you?’

‘I don’t know.’

She said eagerly:

‘Well, I’ll tell you something. In the letter Gwen sent me to say she was coming home – out of the blue – she wrote at the end: “I’m frightened, Elizabeth.” When I tried to ask her she sort of hedged – she was sorry I think that she’d said it. But Gwen – she wouldn’t have said it without a reason…’

‘And you gave the letter to the Inspector, I hope.’

‘Dear God, I burned it. In front of Gwen I burned it. Last night – on the logs in the studio – when we were talking after dinner. It was in my pinafore pocket. I put my pinafore on for washing up and found the letter and just put it on the fire.’ She laughed, an unpleasant sound.

‘But you told them.’

‘Oh, yes, I told them. What Gwen wrote is quoted in my statement. But – they know I want Sammy cleared. What value does it have – a few words out of my head? But I told them other things too. I told them what I could about Gwen’s life in London. That it was very – wild, perhaps. She's taken drugs. I told them. She has the weirdest friends. I've met some of them. Not to know, I don't remember any names. But they've taken her front door key.'

'They'll investigate everything.'

'Are you all right?'

He had hardly been able to speak, and she had noticed. His reaction to her vague description of Gwen in London had sent the blood thudding in his temples with rage, jealousy and despair, had constricted his throat. He had to bring his willpower to bear on his emotions. He got up.

'Yes, thanks. Don't think I slept much, either.' He leaned down to her, his hands on her shoulders. 'I can't *do* anything, Elizabeth. It's all out of my hands. But talk – and sympathy…'

Elizabeth jumped up beside him. 'Tea usually goes with sympathy. Forgive me.'

'Mrs Grice looked after me.'

'Do you think she's all right?'

'You both are. But comfort each other. Be together as much as possible. Your sufferings are the same.' And his. The arrogance of it! 'Shall I come tomorrow?'

'Oh, come tonight, if you can.'

'But you'll be sleeping.'

'I'll try to sleep this afternoon. Rest at least. Come this evening.'

She walked with him to the front door. It

was a glorious morning. A pale settled sunshine was diffused from behind high thin cloud, which was breaking visibly all over to show more and more blue sky. Gwen, who had started the process of decay, Gwen in a drawer in a police mortuary, waiting to be butchered, would have lifted up her chin to this morning, then turned in elation to her sister. Elizabeth gripped Peter King's hand.

'Just help me a moment. Let me hang on.' She dug her fingers into him, hurting. 'It's physical, isn't it, real unhappiness? I've just learned.' She leaned against him, releasing his hand. He was surprised that she still had no woman's impact on him. 'I suppose there'll be post mortems?'

'Almost certainly in Sammy's case. Perhaps in Gwen's too. I should ask them, they'll tell you.' He put his arm around her shoulders. 'It's only bodies…'

'I know.'

'Do you believe they still exist?'

He had seen her sometimes on Sunday mornings, going into the church.

'I – don't – know. I want to. Then I'm afraid it may be wishful thinking. I don't know. Do you?'

'I've always postponed thinking about it. One thing I do believe: it's rather marvellous, really, to be able to say you don't know. The possibilities at least are infinite.'

In all honesty, he could comfort her no

further. But she said:

'I'll go and see poor Mr Melbury. He tried to see me earlier but I couldn't...'

'You go. And on the subject of visits...'

He stopped. He wondered if she had thought of this further burden.

'What?'

'The Press. They'll be on to you.'

'Oh, no!' It was a new idea to her. 'What do I do?'

'You're not obliged to do, or to say, anything. But I would suggest that you're polite.' She would be anyway, probably, even now. 'But don't offer them your theories! Please don't, Elizabeth. Refer them always to the police.'

'Thank you. What will happen now – generally, I mean?'

'Inquests will be opened on them both. And then adjourned.'

'Why adjourned?'

'For police inquiries.'

'Police inquiries? That means ... oh, that means Sammy won't be automatically and publicly proclaimed a murderer!'

'It also means, Elizabeth, that inquiries will be made about Sammy and his capabilities for good or ill, as well as about your sister – and her life. They'll call on your family doctor, on any specialist who treated Sammy...'

Again the laugh he didn't like to hear.

'Gwen dead will become the concern of the country. How much more important to everyone than Gwen alive! It's disgusting. But thanks for preparing me. I know so little...'

'I think you can cope with it. You're strong.' He realised as he offered the comforting words that he believed them.

He glanced back at her from the lane as he walked away. Her face looked bruised as if the assault on her had been physical. In the lane he passed two men, one carrying photographic equipment. They asked him if they were right for Melbury Grange, and he pointed silently behind him.

The onslaught had begun.

7

'Good morning, Miss Hampson.'

The Detective Constable led her forward by the arm, smiling at her. Elizabeth smiled back. She knew him. She knew the Coroner's clerk who was arranging papers on the high table, and the members of the Press now taking their places beneath it, some of whom had paid visits to Melbury Grange. She knew the intricate pattern of the moulding on the ceiling of the Court, and the sense of unreality which descended as she entered.

Three months ago all this had been unknown and now, at the fourth time of assembly, it was a way of life. Elizabeth couldn't remember a time when she was unfamiliar with the layout and procedures and personnel of the Court which sat in the board room of Messrs. Clive and Whicker, solicitors, Great Longford.

But this, the last session, would cost the most. And, once over, it would leave nothing between her and her self-imposed task. Whatever the verdict. Unless … unless the police had made or found a miracle.

Elizabeth looked round at the impassive

faces, heard the faint sounds of last-minute conversations. Everything had the calm of a known and anticipated process. There would be no revelation. The Court would even be able to absorb and nullify her own passion.

Police Constable King, in uniform, alone at the end of the bench near the door, was talking to his opposite number, C.I.D. Elizabeth had been faintly amused all along because of the C.I.D. man's absurd likeness to a detective inspector of television fiction. Soon, doubling as the Coroner's Officer, he would climb to his seat on the dais next to the Coroner, Mr Craig.

Elizabeth looked over at the jury benches, their occupants dribbling in. These men and women were going to assess the significance of the results of the police inquiries for which this inquest on Gwen had been adjourned. Elizabeth had tried to assess it already, in conversation with the C.I.D. She had asked the Detective Inspector if there would be a witness from London. Three months had gone by and they had Gwen's door key. The Detective Inspector gave it back to her and said:

'Nothing material to the case has been brought to light, Miss Hampson. I don't think there will be anything to surprise you tomorrow.'

She said dully:

'I'm sorry I couldn't help you.'

They had taken her to London, gone through Gwen's sparse papers with her (they had gone through them first, of course), and asked her if any names or numbers meant anything to her. None of them did.

But Sammy couldn't have killed Gwen...

The inquest on Sammy had been adjourned too. Only for a fortnight. When it was resumed it numbered among its witnesses the family doctor, a very old retired man who had seen Sammy in a consultant capacity when Sammy was a child, and Aunt Madge. Their statements for the purposes of the inquest were brief. Elizabeth, Mrs Grice and Police Constable King each described their view of Sammy's death. The consultant corroborated the family doctor's opinion that the damage to Sammy's brain in infancy had increased the likelihood of cerebral seizure, particularly after unusual exertion or emotional shock; Aunt Madge recounted an episode in Sammy's youth when he had appeared to have a fit; the Home Office Pathologist reported his findings; and the Coroner with a minimum of wordage brought in a verdict of death from natural causes.

But today... Elizabeth looked again at the jurymen and women. She saw their faces as cold, shuttered. They were carrying out a chore which was something in their diaries between breakfast and lunch. In that space of time they would sum up the capacities of Sammy's life. Without having lived with him and tended him. Without ever having seen him.

Oh, Sammy, I'm glad you're dead. Thank God at least for that.

It would give her something to do on her knees in church on Sunday. Gritsy would be hurt if she didn't go. 'Dear God, thank you for letting Sammy die.' She hadn't anything else to say to God at the moment. And the Sunday after she wouldn't be there…

'Will you please all stand up.'

Was it only the fourth time that she had complied with this request?

The part-time Coroner took his seat with the minimum of fuss. His temporary Officer moved in beside him.

'This is the resumed inquest into the death of Gwendolen Mary Hampson…'

The Coroner's voice was light and gentle, his manner informal inside the ordered framework of his conduct of affairs. Peter King had said to Elizabeth after the opening of the inquest on Sammy:

'We're lucky. You don't always get part-time Coroners of this calibre.'

Elizabeth thought he was a nice man. She saw real concern in the way he looked at her before he started his questions.

Mr Craig went through Elizabeth's

deposition, reading her chunks of it where he could so that she had only to corroborate. Not that she was afraid of the facts. She had taught herself, now, to go through them without readmitting them into more than her most superficial thoughts. But when the Coroner, having brought her to the end of the night Gwen died, turned the last page, removed his spectacles and leaned back in his seat, Elizabeth was afraid – afraid with anguish because her passionate conviction and scant knowledge might not be enough to prevent the events of the night going into the past with Sammy forever recorded as his sister's killer.

One of the female jurors was frowning at a mark on her skirt, beginning to pick at it. Peter King's face was turned towards the witness box, its normal pale and calm. They were the last details Elizabeth saw before the Court dissolved into the blur of her fear.

'Miss Hampson,' said the Coroner kindly, 'can you tell the Court something about the relationship which existed between your sister and your brother – er – Sammy?'

Oh, but she could! Gently now. The thing was, not to say too much, too passionately. Not to appear to be colouring fact into fiction or prejudice.

'My sister and I – with Mrs Grice,' – she nodded through the blur – 'were Sammy's life. I think – I'm sure – that he loved Gwen and me equally. Only – in the last few years she wasn't home much, and so he got excited – thrilled I should say – when she came. He sat through tea – that day – beside her, gazing at her, loving her.' She was managing to talk about it without feeling it. Oh, let it go on that way.

'And – earlier, Miss Hampson. Do you remember any episode in your brother's life when he showed any – belligerence, any tendency to violence – against your sister?'

Elizabeth heard an ugly laugh, then realised it was her own. She was shaken at this evidence that she was not in entire control. A section of the jury suddenly zoomed into focus, she saw the distress in the face of the woman who had seemed to be absorbed with her skirt. The Coroner said:

'Would you like a chair, Miss Hampson? A glass of water?'

The weakness was passing. Slackening her grip on the front of the witness box, Elizabeth said:

'No, thank you, Mr Craig, I'm all right.' She looked across the room. 'Please don't be sorry for me. Just listen to me. I have never seen my brother show any tendency whatsoever to – violence – against my sister, or against anyone or anything else.'

That was the crux of it, and it was out. Quietly and steadily. It made up perhaps for the feebleness of her responses to Mr Craig's gentle but persistent questions about Gwen in London. No, she didn't know any of her sister's friends, although she had met a few of them from time to time. No, she didn't know what relationships, if any, her sister had with people in Town. No, she hadn't met her sister's employers, didn't know what her hobbies were. No. No. No.

'I gather then, Miss Hampson, that when your sister came home – infrequently, as you tell me and as it appears – you did not discuss her life in London?'

'That is so.'

'What did you discuss? What concerned you both?'

'Upper Longford concerned us both. It was my sister's home as well as mine. We had a long shared past. A lifetime.'

They could talk like this for ever and no answers would come. Eventually the Coroner said:

'Is there anything you wish to add in evidence, Miss Hampson, to your statement and to what you have said in response to my questions?'

An awful moment of wasteful silence. She hadn't expected the opportunity. But there were some words in her mind.

'One thing…'

'Yes, Miss Hampson?'

'At the resumed inquest on my brother it was given as medical evidence that the likelihood of cerebral seizure could have been enhanced by unusual exertion or emotional shock. Something like that.'

'Yes, Miss Hampson, that was the expression used.'

The Coroner looked at her keenly, concern swallowed up in anticipation.

'When the medical witnesses say the same thing again today, somebody will draw attention to the possible connexion between the "unusual exertion" of killing my sister, and Sammy's collapse. I would like to draw attention to the possible connexion between his collapse and the words "emotional shock". What I mean is, if each word in that medical evidence weighs…'

'…which we must assume it does, Miss Hampson.'

'Thank you … then my brother is at least *as likely* to have died from emotional shock (which could have been the passive shock of seeing murder done or discovering it), as from unusual exertion.'

As Elizabeth ended she realised she was in full focus with the room, and that one of the male jurors was taking notes. The Press were scribbling non-stop, a tableful of them, most of the men in light jackets, a woman in shocking pink. They were the one piece of colour in the room, the jury were as soberly clad as the witnesses. Peter King's head, which had focused in profile, turned quickly to look at her, and she thought she noticed fleeting approval.

'Thank you, Miss Hampson. Is that all you wish to say?'

'Just one other thing, if I may.'

'Yes?'

'I wish simply to emphasise that the french window into the studio, where my sister died, was unlocked.'

'Thank you, Miss Hampson, you have stated this fact in your deposition, and we have been over it. Thank you. That is all.'

Elizabeth found she was glad of a detective's arm to help her back to her seat. Her legs seemed to be locked straight at the knees. She had perhaps, in the end, been out of line. Would it have been better to have been really out of line by crying out to them that Sammy couldn't have killed Gwen, throwing off her imposed calm?

Perhaps she would have done so, it was what her instinct wanted, if Peter King hadn't said, just as they went in, a hand on her arm like a restraint:

'Remember, Elizabeth, the french window was unlocked.'

That was all he had said, but she had taken it as a warning against special pleading. And although she might not need facts, strangers, justice-makers, did…

Mrs Grice had begun her evidence. Peter King was watching the witness box, as expressionless as ever. At the end, and with much dignity, Mrs Grice said to the Coroner's invitation:

'It is my opinion that Sammy did not kill his sister.'

'Why do you say that, Mrs Grice?'

'Because, sir, observing him through the whole of his life' – she faltered for the only time– 'I am convinced that he had no violence in him.'

'Thank you very much, Mrs Grice.'

The jury looked with universal favour on Mrs Grice as she stood down.

Peter King went into the witness box.

Elizabeth was surprised to find that she now had to strive to keep attentive. She wanted to go to sleep. The feeling of unreality which had come and gone like a saving presence during each of the sessions in this room engulfed her again. For the moment it was all a dream and she would not pinch herself to wake up, because when she found she had to go on dreaming it would turn into a nightmare – the nightmare of sitting in public chewing over the violent deaths of the two people who made up her life...

'You were off duty, but you had gone up to Melbury Grange for' – the Coroner studied the papers in front of him– 'a last check and to give your dog the opportunity of a run.'

Peter King said:

'That is correct.'

'You had left the village at approximately 11.50 p.m., and reached Melbury Grange about two minutes before you heard the screaming... It seems, Police Constable King, that it took you fifteen minutes to complete this short walk...'

'I had eaten too much...'

A laugh like a sigh drifted across the court. Elizabeth resented it, then remembered that she herself had laughed a few times in the past months. And these were strangers.

Peter King's evidence was a mixture of procedure and self-defence. He reported the fact of the murder and the process of handing it over; and he tried to say what he had been doing in the vicinity of the crime. Absurdly, between the evidence of the Police Constable and the Detective Inspector, Ted Harkness was called to corroborate that Peter King had supped with him and had left at 11.50 p.m. in full possession of his faculties.

Elizabeth thought there was a suggestion of stir among the Press when the Police Constable said that someone might have left by the french window while he was fumbling at the gate.

Ted Harkness had to be cut short in each of his replies. The Detective Inspector said what was expected of him. Then they called Aunt Madge.

Elizabeth was jolted out of her dream. She hadn't noticed Aunt Madge at the end of the row, and Aunt Madge hadn't sought recognition. Elizabeth thought she knew why when Aunt Madge gave evidence that Sammy had once, and with violence, pulled her hair.

'Shrivelled bitch,' said Elizabeth, for Mrs Grice to hear. Mrs Grice squeezed Elizabeth's hand, lying in the space between them. Aunt Madge took her skinny self back into the corner where she was blocked out again by the bulk of the family doctor.

But on the stand the family doctor said he understood Aunt Madge, and it was his opinion that Sammy had a definite capacity for violence, if frustrated, which might never manifest itself but which was nevertheless there.

'What conclusions then, Dr Jones, have you reached as to the cause of this woman's death?'

'In view of the circumstantial evidence, and my knowledge of her brother's conditions and capabilities, I maintain it is possible she met her death by his hand.'

The aged consultant said much the same thing and the Press went on scribbling and the jury went on looking alert. Evidence was offered on the inquest into the death of Sammy. The Home Office Pathologist gave evidence that Gwen had died by the penetration of a knife into her liver, and that was that.

Elizabeth looked round the Court. The last witnesses, so reliable, so obscenely wrong, had tired her almost to that longed-for sleep. And they were the last. No witnesses from London. Nobody standing by in Melbury Lane as Peter King fumbled at the gate. No footmarks but his on the grass, no marks on the path from the french window – although it had been submitted by the police that, in view of the weather, footmarks on the path would not necessarily have left a trace.

Mr Craig swept a glance round the Court. Every face was looking towards him. He took off his spectacles, sighed, and sat back. There was a moment of silence, while attention deepened. The intermittent sun had travelled to a point where, emerging from a cloud, it burst into the Court room in a furry shaft that went straight to the witnesses' eyes.

Elizabeth heard Mr Craig begin his summing up before the sun faded and she could see him.

'Ladies and gentlemen of the jury,' said Mr Craig, and some of the jurymen and women shifted slightly in their seats to acknowledge his direct address. 'You now have before you such evidence as it has been possible to assemble...' His voice came and went in Elizabeth's consciousness. She struggled to attend.

'...I would remind you that the person known as Sammy is not before the Court, that in view of his death no evidence could be taken of his mental condition following the death of this woman... I would remind you that no one saw the act of murder committed...' Oh, but imagination needed no reminders! '...that it is physically possible for another person or persons to have been on the scene at the time of the murder and to have left it undetected ... remind you, in short, that no evidence given in this case is entirely conclusive.'

The sun came again, cutting off the face of the Coroner from the witnesses, lulling Elizabeth further into her exhausted calm.

'It is, however, clear that the circumstantial evidence points strongly in one direction, but before arriving at a verdict towards which that evidence points you must be satisfied beyond any reasonable doubt that this woman died by her brother's hand. Anything less than this is not sufficient for a verdict against him. If you feel confident and certain that the brother did kill the sister, you must say so. If you are not satisfied you must say that she was murdered by a person or persons unknown.'

As the sun faded, the figure of the Coroner slowly reappeared before Elizabeth's dazzled sleepy eyes. He was leaning forward now, speaking slowly and with emphasis, all his attention on the jury so that Elizabeth saw only a half profile. Peter King had said the Coroner would show them as clearly as he could where the proper verdict lay, and he was doing so. He might think Sammy was guilty, but he didn't feel the evidence was conclusive enough to direct them to such a verdict. An honest man. A fair one. He was even putting the possibilities to them again.

'…if you are satisfied that this woman was in fact murdered by her brother…'

Ah, no!

There was a clattering sound and the sun exploded in a hail of sparks, surrounding Elizabeth with warmth. She expanded into it. Was comfortable for the first time she could remember. She moved her limbs luxuriously. She heard small grunting sounds and realised, like a laugh she had once heard somewhere, that they were her own. There were other sounds: persistent whispering voices and one louder voice, going on and on like a refrain. She started to listen to it.

'Elizabeth. Elizabeth. How are you now? How are you?'

She opened her eyes. Peter King's face was just in front of hers, looking anxious. With a sickening lurch she realised that to bend her head towards him she must raise it, that she was lying down. The room swung and juddered as she adjusted. It was not the Court room. The ceiling was low and unadorned, an unshaded light bulb hung above her. She turned her head from side to side, slowly, and saw legs and one or two people crouched, watching her. She flexed her fingers and felt wool. Peter King was still there. He seemed to know what she wanted, and came round and put his hands under her head. Her body was spread out in front of her, covered with a rug. Mrs Grice appeared over her chest and took her hand.

'It's all right,' said Mrs Grice and Peter King together, and Elizabeth chuckled.

'That's a better sound,' said Mrs Grice. Peter King had found some sort of cushion, and pushed it under her head.

'What happened?'

'The strain…' said Mrs Grice, stroking Elizabeth's hand.

'You fainted,' said Peter King, 'dead away.'

'Oh, no!' She remembered the clatter, which she had heard as a far off sound. Again she had failed to take the measure of herself. When would she be in command again? She had always been in command.

'Is it over?'

Peter King squatted on the floor beside her.

'It's over.'

'Tell me.'

'Murder against person or persons unknown.' He watched her impassive face. 'It was the best we could expect.'

'I know, I know. Did the jury retire?'

'Not for very long.'

'But they did. How long have I been here?'

'About half an hour.'

A strange doctor appeared above her and Peter King and Mrs Grice went out of view. He took hold of Elizabeth's wrist. She looked down at her arm, realising it hurt. The sleeve was back and there was a red dot inside a bruise.

'You gave me an injection.'

'You're all right now.' He smiled at her. 'You've been too strong.'

'I'm very weak.'

'I don't think so. You can go home. So long as you let Police Constable King drive your car.'

The doctor and Peter King helped her to her feet. A century separated her from the deaths of Gwen and Sammy, unbridgeably, and she was grateful.

'You must rest for a while.'

'Just for a while.'

She knew what she still had to do.

PART TWO

ELIZABETH

8

People in Upper Longford, when they heard Elizabeth was going to London, tended to tell her that she would obviously clear things up as quickly as possible and get back home. Elizabeth smiled at them, not answering.

She chose to travel on a day when Peter King was off duty, so that he could go with her. He had offered to.

Elizabeth took with her some work she had done in the months since Gwen and Sammy died. She had set about it in the usual way, when she abandoned Gwen's portrait, but it had taken a new turn. At the beginning it had been a chore, which she had welcomed as possible therapy, and then suddenly she had found a sort of demonic inspiration. Instead of starting after breakfast and finishing at tea time, in her old tempered way, she had worked into the summer darkness and even got up to work during the night.

That was why she was taking the result with her – three paintings and a handful of drawings – to offer to a new London market. Peter King had seen them and found them exciting. It astonished him that they were so much more exciting than Elizabeth herself. He even dreamed about them one night. He had encouraged her to take them to Town. He said to her on the train:

'After all, you can't spend all the time...'

Then tailed off. They had so far avoided finding a title for Elizabeth's purpose in London.

Though Elizabeth found she had instincts of unkindness, now, towards some people, they never included Peter King. He had helped her, perhaps vitally, She knew she affected him no more than she had ever done, but he had helped her. She thought it was out of his vocational self, and was impressed and touched by his putting of himself at her disposal. She was glad she had no more disposition to love him than he to love her, and so was not tempted to misunderstand his motives. It was enough, it was enormous, that he made life easier.

So she tried to help him out.

'Being Gwen?' she suggested.

'Is that it?'

'Isn't it? I've got to think and feel myself into her life, steadily, all the time. So being Elizabeth taking pictures to a gallery won't help the process.'

'It will keep you sane. Promise me you'll go.'

'Oh, I'll go.'

Peter King lost his footing in the slops of

beer and tea on the floor of the buffet car. Elizabeth saved him from falling and they both laughed. Hers was a mild deep chuckle that reassured him. He carried tea through to the adjoining coach, pushing bottles and cans across a sticky table top to make room.

'Have you got the paper I gave you?'

'The precious paper? Of course I have.'

Peter King had told his opposite number, C.I.D., that Elizabeth wanted to meet people in London who had known her sister, and the Detective Constable had had only initial hesitation in handing over a list of names, addresses and telephone numbers.

'They're all in her book, anyway, but lost among hordes of others that don't lead anywhere. Not that these lead very far. An uncommunicative lot! Not my idea of friends. Anyway, this'll save her wasting time.'

Elizabeth told Peter King she had all the time in the world. But the list would be somewhere to begin. It was quite short.

Elizabeth knew it by heart but opened it again over the tea.

'Can these be all the friends Gwen had?'

'They're probably all the people she knew well.' The pain came and went. 'If that. From what I've heard of your sister's life in London – relationships didn't last long, or go very deep.'

'No.' Elizabeth looked out at the countryside, like Peter King resisting pain. The thick glass was filthy, thin dashes of rain were appearing diagonally across it, not clearing it, forming a second barrier between her and the colourless landscape. But it was a time for barriers to come down.

'What am I trying to do?'

She wasn't really speaking to him, but he said:

'Find out more than the police did! But you have certain advantages.' She looked at him. 'Because you're *not* the police. People should talk to you more easily, be less on their guard. And – you're the twin, you're half way to understanding now – even if you don't know it.'

'Oh, I don't know it. I didn't *understand* Gwen – I probably never did. Nor she me. But that was the least important thing. You don't have to understand something to be part of it.'

'You're right, of course. Who understands the universe?'

'Tell me.' Elizabeth drained her plastic cup. 'Do you think I'm wasting my time? You've never really said. If you do, is it because you think I won't find what's to be found? Or because there's nothing to find? That – Sammy… I've never asked you. I'd like to know.'

He looked into her face, tense for his reply behind its slight smile. Colour had come back under the skin, order was restored to the hair, the dress, but she didn't look quite the same person she had been before. Peter King would have been hard put to it to define the difference, but he thought it was summed up in her mouth. Elizabeth was less certain of things.

He had not succeeded in solving his own small puzzle in Gwen's death, that he was not even sure, all the time, existed. He said:

'I don't know. There's something. I told you at the beginning there was something…'

He had spent some time trying to find out what that something was. When he concentrated on it too precisely it disappeared.

'It's something I can't put my finger on, yet something I feel is terribly obvious. It's this – plus your conviction.'

She looked pleased. 'You can stay the night, by the way,' she said, 'if you change your mind about going back tonight. There are two bedrooms.'

'Thanks, but I'll take the overnight train. I'm on duty in the morning.'

He smiled at her politely, thinking how Gwen wouldn't, couldn't have said that. Even if she hadn't wanted him in her bed, she would have given a soufflé-light provocation to her denial of him. How would Elizabeth cope in Gwen's world? He felt a wave of protective pity for her.

'I'll come up again next week-end. Take a piece of holiday.'

'Will you? Oh, I'll be glad if you will.'

She was slightly less ladylike. It had, once, been as unthinkable that they could be friends as lovers.

The building which housed the flat had a lush lobby with palms and sofas and a uniformed commissionaire. The flat, reached by one in a row of carpeted lifts and a wide warm corridor, might have been the show flat for a very trendy through scheme got up for a colour supplement feature.

They moved silently about the sitting-room.

'Do you remember it?' asked Peter King at last.

'No.' Elizabeth looked round in a sort of bewilderment. 'I never really noticed it, except that I didn't like the pictures. Gwen – was here.'

There was nothing for either of them. Elizabeth sank wearily into a chair, that looked like nothing so much as a gouged tomato.

'It's comfortable!' she said, trying to laugh.

'There'll be drink here at least,' said Peter King.

'That's how I feel: "at least". Yes, I do remember that, I think. The cupboard near the window, if the police have left any.'

'Naughty,' reproved Peter King. The effortful badinage helped them slightly. He gave her brandy.

'Have some yourself,' murmured Elizabeth. The spirit seared her chest. It appeared to help.

'Thank you, ma'am.'

She joined him at the window. The view was mainly chimney pots, a near and distant prospect of them, the remains of old Chelsea beneath the new, where they stood on a sixth floor.

'I'll have to talk to that man at the desk downstairs.'

It was a hatefully unwelcome prospect, and it was only a start. Peter King saw her thoughts in her face. He put his arm round her shoulders.

'Remember, Elizabeth, that the police have done it all, already.'

'They weren't her sister. You said so yourself.'

It sounded an emptily defiant remark in that place of no clues.

'I know. I just want you to remember the odds against us.'

'Against *us?*'

'Well, yes.'

'Thank you!'

Her grateful smile transformed her face, but gave him a moment of guilt. He really didn't know how far he would have supported her, at the beginning, if it hadn't been for Gwen. But now, for whatever reason, the team was made up.

He let her go alone into Gwen's bedroom. She closed the door and sat down on the bed, waiting.

'Same old car,' said Gwen. 'I had to come.'

But you didn't have to die.

Elizabeth sat with clenched fists, glaring round the room.

'Most of us, darling, need a prop for most of the time. We can't support ourselves.'

I can't support this.

But I must. It has happened.

In a series of quick angry movements, Elizabeth jumped up from the bed, tore open the wardrobe, and ruffled from end to end of Gwen's dresses. Gwen's scent floated from among them, and Elizabeth went to the door and called Peter King.

'Sleep next door!' he said, alarmed at her face.

Elizabeth drew away from him, twitching her pony-tail.

'No. I'm all right now.'

Carefully she prepared to go out. By the time she was ready she felt the worst might be over.

They sat in a restaurant until it was time for Peter to go for his train. Bizarrely dressed people came and went in the gloom. Elizabeth and Peter thought they were the only pair not to greet or be greeted on arrival.

'Gwen probably knew half of them. Peter,

it's going to be like the proverbial needle!'

'Work on the names we've given you. And your instincts.'

She wasn't listening.

'But, Peter, if they'd known Gwen, these people – any people – wouldn't they at least half look at me?'

'You're not really alike.'

'We're identical!'

Peter King thought of Mrs Grice. 'It depends what you see.'

He took her as far as the lush foyer, and left her. Another uniformed man now sat behind the desk. Pulses started to beat in Elizabeth's temples. She walked up to the desk and the man looked at her, puzzled.

'Good evening,' said Elizabeth tremulously, 'I'm Miss Hampson's twin sister.'

The man's face cleared.

'Of course! You're very alike, aren't you? And yet…'

Elizabeth was used to this kind of reaction. In a way it was her own. She said:

'I've come to wind up here.'

'We were all shocked. A dreadful business.'

'Yes. I shall take my time. As you'll appreciate, I want to meet people who knew my sister. I want to talk to them.' It was as if a shutter was sliding down over his eyes. 'But where on earth do I start? A few names in an address book.'

The eyes now were totally blank, wide and

determinedly frank. The man said:

'The police will tell you who's who.'

'They won't, you know. Their investigations up here were – rather formal.'

'You surprise me, madam. They questioned us enough.'

Here it was already. The police had found nothing, but had left behind them suspicion, the old fear of involvement. Please, miss, it wasn't me!

Elizabeth said wearily:

'And me too.' She sought his sympathy. 'It was terrible...'

The eyes softened, lost some of their wariness.

'I'm so sorry. I hope the flat won't upset you.'

'I'll be all right. Though it is a bit tricky...' She smiled bravely.

'Let us know if there's anything you want. My mate and I – that's Reg, you may have seen him earlier...'

'Yes, I saw him.'

'One of us is always on. You can ring down. I'm George, by the way.'

'Thanks, George. I'll be glad to know you're here.'

As soon as she got upstairs Elizabeth telephoned Mrs Grice. The warm steady voice went through her like brandy, filling her with a nostalgia for home which she repulsed vigorously as inappropriate for the moment and – as something she should resist now that Gwen was no longer there to balance her. A sort of staidness?

'Have you had a meal, Elizabeth?'

'Yes, darling, I have. Spaghetti with background – all sorts and conditions of colourful young and not so young.'

'Near the flat? Is the flat aired?'

'The flat's aired and the restaurant is just around the corner. Gwen must have known it. It's a task, Gritsy.'

'Don't feel you have to solve it.'

'I'm not looking to the end of it. I don't know what I expect out of it. At the moment – the job's the thing.' A voyage of discovery into the interior as well as outwards with the ripples of the dropped stone. 'All well with you? How's Ginger's ear?'

'He didn't take so well to the drops. But he's been more comfortable since. I'm quite all right.'

'Peter will come and see you in the morning.'

'I'll look forward to that.'

Elizabeth was tired, but before she went to bed she looked through every drawer and cupboard in the flat. She wanted to find out the worst confrontation that awaited her, so that she would not dream of the unknown. She suspected that everything was a good deal tidier than it would have been before the police went through it.

The process wasn't as painful as she had dreaded, but much more sad: there was so little tangible evidence in Gwen's drawers of the accretions of a personality – so few snapshots, bits of paper, letters, programmes, cards.

Only near the end of her search, wrapped in an old woollen vest, at the very back and bottom of a drawer, was a large photograph of Alan. There it was suddenly as the wrapping fell away, smiling up at Elizabeth with the impact of a sudden entry into the room.

It made her cry. She had identified Alan to the police from a snapshot at Melbury Grange and told them how long since he'd left England, and they hadn't shown her this large studio photograph. They'd just returned it, in its chosen cover, to its place.

For a long time Elizabeth sat on the end of the bed, the square of cardboard dangling between her knees, crying at her discovery that Gwen had carried her betrayal into her anaesthetising London world.

When she was too tired to cry any more she wrapped the photograph up again and put it away.

She pulled out the drawer above and looked down at the sprawl of cosmetics. Automatically she opened the large powder compact, and stared for a moment's incomprehension at its contents. Then she dropped it back as if it burned her and slammed the drawer shut.

As she lay beyond sleep in the darkness her thoughts of Gwen gave way to uneasy astonishment at herself and what seemed all at once like her isolation in a lusty world.

9

Elizabeth's few hours of sleep came late. It was nine in the morning when she finally awoke, because this high corner of a city was quieter than the countryside which for unbroken years had lain outside her window. Up here, the traffic and the business of the streets was an unpunctuated hum. Inside this building, with its unimaginable ranks of eaters, lovers, quarrellers, ablutors, the plumbing was of impeccable modernity and no outside foot could fall nearer than the thickly carpeted corridor.

When her thoughts began to grow too menacing, Elizabeth got out of bed and went to the window, drawing the curtains back on a sky view, pale blue and streaked with wisps of cirrus. A cat, arrested in its purpose on a roof ridge below, looked up at her reproachfully, holding its acrobatic pose so frozenly that she had to watch and wait until it at last flicked a back leg and resumed its steady prowl.

It was the only evidence of nature, beyond that large bland sky.

Elizabeth dressed and ate her imported provisions with her thoughts in conscious abeyance. She tidied up, made some telephone calls, found a carrier bag, and prepared to go out. In the sitting-room doorway she turned round for what she recognised as a last plea to the flat to help her.

It failed. She simply couldn't believe that Gwen had chosen these carefully balanced ingredients of current living trends. Gwen had stepped into something ready prepared for person or persons unknown. That, surely, was what Gwen was in London – as was her assailant in Upper Longford.

Elizabeth banged the door.

Reg was in the lobby. He was as wary as George and no more helpful, except in similar offers of practical assistance. To approach him was already less of a terror.

'Where are the best shops for food?'

'At the back.' Reg waved a hand away from the main doors. 'A street of them. All you'll want.'

The shops were in a row, the ground floors of an eighteenth century terrace, effectively opposing their small-scale colour and diversity to the vast glassy prestige stretch opposite, from which Elizabeth emerged into the funnelled wind.

There seemed to be one shop of each kind, which might simplify her task.

Elizabeth, hesitating, saw one elderly woman behind the bakery counter, and went in. She watched for a reaction, but there was only a widening of the kindly, expectant smile.

'Yes, ducky?'

Elizabeth bought a loaf. She asked the woman if she knew Gwendolen Hampson, and described Gwen with reference to herself. The woman couldn't help her. The same process, the same lack of reaction, at the greengrocer's, the grocer's, and the butcher's. She bought provisions.

The next façade was a ladies' hairdresser, and in the window, caught and vivified by the sun, was Gwen, head back, pale hair gleaming.

'A-a-ah!'

A young man inside heard her, and caught her as she swayed in the open doorway. Elizabeth looked in terror into his close concerned face.

'Think you can make that chair?'

She nodded and moved inside his friendly arm, shielded from the horror in the window. She was sitting down, banging her head on the dryer that hung above the seat, not feeling it because of the numbness of shock.

'What is it, then, dear?'

She got it out at last, and at last he persuaded her to go with him to the window. They stood looking down on the polystyrene head, topped with its pale gleaming wig.

'I'm sorry.' She laughed shakily. It was the best introduction she could have had, if costly. 'My sister was called Gwen Hampson. Do you do the hair of a Miss Gwen Hampson?'

There was no reaction in his face but he said:

'I'll see.'

He put her back in the chair and left her. This time the dryer hurt, bobbing back on to her ear. Another young man approached her. Same height, same infinitesimal hips, same length of leg. The age bred a certain shape. The age in London, at least.

'Miss Hampson? I'm Robert.'

She looked up the length of him. His face was embarrassed for her. 'We were all so shattered…' It was extravagantly camp but it was genuine. Of course. There was the horrible complication of the murderer probably being in the family. It clouded people's sympathy, stopped it from being a straightforward emotion.

But he knew. Elizabeth got up. The young man was still high above her. She said eagerly:

'You did her hair…'

'The last few times. Her regular stylist, Rupert, he's left us.'

'I want to meet people who maybe knew her a little.' The most natural thing in the world, but the wide eyes dropped. Mr

Robert coughed behind his hand. 'Would you have his address?'

There was a moment of silence.

'Please!'

He said: 'I think I can let you have it.' Elizabeth followed him to the desk at the back. 'The police, you know,' he said vaguely, 'It's upsetting...'

She agreed with him. He wrote on a piece of paper, and handed it to Elizabeth. She put it into her bag. She thanked him and he said 'Any time' but she thought he was glad to see her go. Actually, she got no further than the doorway, because after forcing herself to look once more at the pale blonde head, she went back into the shop and spoke to Mr Robert again.

In the street a sun shaft covered a table and chair outside a pub. When Elizabeth came out of the hairdressers she sat down in the sunshine. It was lunchtime, and Gritsy never let her go without lunch. But nor did she drink spirits at midday, and today she looked at the ugly building opposite over a glass of whisky instead of ordering food. She tried to find her window among the high rows of small squares that topped the prestigious glass, but there was no way of being sure.

Afterwards she went to see the photographer who had launched Gwen and with whom Gwen worked exclusively. She gained nothing beyond some praise of Gwen and the now familiar embarrassed condolences. He and his whole team had been on an assignment in Yugoslavia – Gwen had taken her holiday to coincide with it.

The photographer and his staff were terribly kind, but terribly busy. The photographer punctuated his conversation with Elizabeth by encouraging words to an artificially windswept model and the clicking of his camera. When he was called away he told both Elizabeth and the model that he'd be back, but Elizabeth didn't wait. She went reluctantly back to the flat, where, defying the isolation and the silence, she telephoned a Mayfair gallery and arranged to take her work along.

At a quarter past seven a parcel was delivered to her by hand, and at half past Miss Wendy Tiller, of Kensington, came to see her as requested. Miss Tiller was small and dark and plump and very pretty. She wriggled in her seat when Elizabeth, looking out of the window, said:

'Wendy, were you really Gwen's friend?'

Elizabeth didn't look round during the pause.

'Well, of course… I mean, we saw each other, sort of regularly. And we never bitched. That was just luck, I suppose, but we didn't. We went out together. When we could find free nights at the same time.'

Wendy giggled. 'What do you mean, anyway?'

Elizabeth turned round, making a decision.

'I mean. I'm wondering if you can help me. You see, I didn't know her very well lately. But I knew our brother, and I know he didn't kill her.'

Wendy smiled uncertainly. Elizabeth sat down on the floor in front of her. She noticed that Wendy's eyeshadow was geared for more distant viewing and that she had an obvious false tooth.

'You read all the accounts in the papers, I suppose?' Wendy nodded. 'The french window wasn't locked,' said Elizabeth, 'and I'm not satisfied. Who in London might have wanted to kill her?' She waited resignedly for the shutter to come down over the gobbily fringed eyes.

'I told the police I couldn't help them.'

'Just tell me about Gwen.'

Wendy recrossed her legs. Elizabeth backed slightly away, giving her room.

'She didn't talk about herself, really. Well, hardly at all. You know – I was the one who talked!' Wendy laughed at herself in surprised discovery, making Elizabeth like her.

'Don't you remember any names?'

'Only Rupert...'

Rupert. Elizabeth reached for her bag nearby on the floor and found the small slip of paper. She read the name Rupert Baxter, with an address and telephone number. On the other piece of paper, the one Peter King had given her, was the name R.J. Baxter, with the same telephone number and address.

Elizabeth said:

'He did her hair…'

'And the rest! Oh, sorry, darling.' Elizabeth had visibly flinched. 'But you wanted to know.'

'Yes.' Elizabeth put the two papers back in her handbag and got to her feet. 'I did want to know, thanks. Anyone else?'

She was braced now but Wendy only said:

'Can't think.' She looked at Elizabeth's pleading face, and began obviously concentrating. 'Oh, yes! I actually met someone here once. When we were drowning our sorrows one night. A big sulky bear rang the bell. Gwen brought him in but he was so growly she told him to go away after about five minutes.'

'And?'

'He went. Sort of hunched his shoulders at her – and went. Didn't say a word. God, I didn't remember, I didn't tell them. You don't think…? It seemed – forgive me, dear, but it seemed as if one didn't have to look as far as London…'

'I know. What was this man's name?'

'I'm a fool, darling, I ought to remember.

She talked about him sometimes after that. Sort of laughing at him.'

'Laughing?'

'Well, yes. But that's not quite right. Oh, she did laugh but I used to feel – as if she didn't want to, as if she almost liked him very much and was sort of angry with him that she couldn't like him more still. As if he wouldn't let her.'

'And Rupert?'

'Oh, he was a sort of current thing. She subbed him.'

'Subbed?' Shuddery thoughts of the gratification of weird desires.

'Oh, sorry. Gave him money, I'm afraid.'

'Why?'

Wendy shrugged. It was like that childhood shrug of Gwen's.

'For the time being she wanted him. And he wanted money.'

'I thought hairdressers got lots of money.'

'He had expensive tastes. Sports cars, and so on. And...'

'Yes. Go on, please.'

'Other birds.'

'Oh, no!'

'Darling,' said Wendy helplessly. 'Only part of Gwen was involved. There was always the other part of her that stood aside, sort of commenting.'

Elizabeth began to respect Wendy.

'Was she frightened of him?'

'You're joking, of course. She had this thing going for him. So he had a certain temporary power. Strictly temporary, I'm sure.' There was a pause. Elizabeth felt tired, confused. The light was waning. Wendy said at last, leaning forward:

'I think she was a bit afraid of Thomas.'

'Thomas?'

'Oh, God, that's his name, isn't it? You always get a thing when you're not trying for it. Thomas. That's the bear.'

'And Gwen was afraid of him?'

I'm frightened, Elizabeth.

'I think – in some weird way – she was afraid of him disapproving.'

'Gwen?'

'As ever was. But it's only a feeling I've got.'

Elizabeth already respected Wendy's feelings. She brought out the list, but there was no initial T.

'Would you like a drink?'

'I was wondering when you'd ask.'

Elizabeth rested over her whisky while Wendy talked about herself. She made Elizabeth think of stools at bar counters and women assessing talent through lack-lustre eyes. Of Gwen doing that. When Wendy got up to go, two drinks later, she asked her, with a last despairing thrust:

'Can't you think of anything else? Anything else at all? Anything – out of the ordinary?'

Wendy considered a moment, then burst out laughing.

'Only church.'

'Church?'

'That's what I said. Sometimes when we tried to fix a date Gwen would say she couldn't because of going to church. Sometimes she'd say – what would she say? – she'd say "When I was going to church the other night..." I remember once asking her if she was a Catholic. If she'd been a Catholic, it wouldn't have seemed... Catholics are Catholics whatever ... well, you know.'

'I know. But she wasn't a Catholic.'

'So she said. But that was all. So it stuck with me. Sort of kinky. I mean, I couldn't see Gwen on a flower rota, or polishing the pots for Easter.'

Neither could Elizabeth. Gwen never came to church on her week-ends home in Upper Longford.

Wendy put a plump kind hand on her shoulder.

'Are you all right? Shall I stay a bit?'

Elizabeth was all at once dying to be rid of her.

'No, I'm all right. Thanks for coming.'

'Any time.'

Elizabeth wasn't inclined to put the easy phrase to the test, any more than with Mr Robert.

When Wendy had gone she emptied the

ashtray and made a telephone call. She said firmly to the man's voice that answered:

'Rupert Baxter, please.'

'Just a minute.'

There were snatches of sound, thumps, whispers. Eventually a lighter voice said, musically:

'Rupert Baxter here.'

Elizabeth said:

'Please don't hang up. I'm Gwen Hampson's sister and I'd like to see you. If you don't come here I shall come to you even without an invitation because I so much want to see you.'

She had to stop there, to draw breath. After a tiny pause the voice at the other end said, caressingly:

'What's the fuss? I'll come. Where are you?'

'At Gwen's.' She was ready for a reaction and thought she heard it, in the slightest catch of breath. 'Will you come tomorrow night?'

'I'll come tomorrow night, Gwen's sister.'

'My name is Elizabeth. About seven o'clock?'

'About seven o'clock, Elizabeth.'

'Thank you.' She waited. There was no further sound. She hung up.

Dusk was stealing about the room. She remained for a few moments at the desk watching it, the dark blue square of sky, the two empty tumblers, the receding violence of the shapes and colours around her. It was a terrible time of day, alone in London.

Elizabeth threw on a coat and went down in the lift. Reg greeted her cheerfully, no longer afraid of her.

Wind fought her as she pushed the doors open, and opposed her the length of the street. At the end of it was the sooty island of St Saviour, its Victorian gothic spire shading off towards the third floor of the flats.

Now as she pressed the door the wind gusted her inwards and she fell across the threshold. Someone was playing the organ softly and a woman was replacing tired carnations on the altar.

A tall figure in black came briskly down a side aisle and Elizabeth went up to him and put her hand on his sleeve. He looked at her and invited her without comment into the vestry. There in answer to her question he told her, with reference to some ledgers, that Miss Gwendolen Hampson was not a spinster of his parish. Nor did he recognise through Elizabeth a member of his congregation. But perhaps she herself would like to come along on Sunday morning?

'It won't tell you about your sister, Miss Hampson, but it may be of some small comfort...'

Elizabeth turned away from him and walked out of the vestry, amazed that she could be so rude. She sat in a pew until the last of the light faded from behind the hectic east window, formulating a series of Christian *cris de coeur* which she couldn't utter.

The vicar passed her several times, but let her alone.

10

The second day began as unproductively as the first. Elizabeth got nowhere with Gwen's dentist, with the church in the other direction (still C of E, there were limits), with the names and addresses.

Still courting disappointment, but of a different kind, in the afternoon she took her painting to the Fromen Gallery.

A young man with exquisite manners propped them in a row against the wall, and stood looking at them.

'Can you leave these with me?'

'Yes … yes, of course I can.'

He asked for her address and telephone number. She had to look them up.

'We'll be in touch.'

He showed her out, and she went back to the flat. It was like losing her identity. Elizabeth stood defiantly in the centre of the sitting-room, glaring round her. She fell with frantic relief on the telephone when it rang.

Peter King's voice asked her if she was all right.

'Better for hearing you,' said Elizabeth. 'Solitary dusk in London is different from Upper Longford.'

'Have you been there alone a long time?'

'Only a few minutes, I'm glad to say.'

'Anything happening?'

'I've had two pointers to one name, and he's coming here tonight.'

'Be careful!'

He sounded worried, and she laughed. She had never thought of being worried for that kind of reason.

'I'll be all right.'

'I can come up on Sunday, if you like.'

'Oh, I wish you would! Can you stay? Can I book you a room somewhere?'

'I'll sleep at home. Time I did.'

When they had finished talking Elizabeth snapped on all the lights. She got ready for Rupert then went to the window with a stiff scotch. An excited group of swallows was disappearing across the serrated orange sea below her. The sky was cloudless, bright dark blue.

How did you feel, darling, when you waited for Rupert? How did it begin – with words, or merely with gestures?

Elizabeth saw it as beginning with a nod of the head, and instant understanding. She knew there were currents of understanding between men and women, working beneath and independent of words, operating on wavelengths she could never discover. There had been teenage holidays where she and Gwen would sit talking to a boy they had just met, talking about the weather and the hotel and the food, Elizabeth thought, and suddenly he and Gwen would get up at the same moment and start dancing closely together, leaving Elizabeth in polite mid-sentence.

She took a long drink into the sudden return of her self-doubt, and went to look at herself in the mirror. Well, it was initial shock effect she was aiming for, and he would get that.

When the bell rang, Elizabeth went and opened the door and stood there, her glass in her hand.

She hardly noticed what the man looked like because of what he did. He swayed against the side of the door, leaned there for an instant, then slid down until he was sitting on the floor with his legs out in front of him. His enormous violet eyes snapped shut when he was half-way to the ground.

Elizabeth was terrified of her success. She patted his nearest white cheek, then the other as his head lolled away from her. His hair and face were almost the same colour. She thought that in her panic she stepped on the long tips of his fingers, but this failed to animate him.

Elizabeth ran into the sitting-room and slopped some brandy into a glass. She heard him muttering as she stumbled back to him, spilling some. She had poured lavishly, in her fright, and he drank it fast, shuddering between each mouthful.

Elizabeth took the glass from him as he drained it. He closed his eyes again and leaned back, but the next moment he was on his feet, standing close beside her, the widest part of his multi-coloured tie on a level with her eyes. The current London shape.

She thought, before looking up to his face, he moves fast, it would have to have been someone moving fast who could have got away from Peter King...

The violet eyes were less wide, wary but no longer scared. In fact he laughed, too high-pitched for Elizabeth's taste.

'Thank God I knew there was a twin.'

'For a moment you forgot.'

Elizabeth went into the sitting-room and sat down in the least comfortable chair.

'As you say.'

He sat down opposite, or rather he was suddenly in a chair, slouching, his bottom on the edge of it, his legs across the carpet and his feet only a few inches from her.

Elizabeth drew hers closer to her in a gesture she knew must look prim as soon as she had instinctively made it. She was herself again, but she didn't think it mattered now.

'You're not really like Gwen.'

She didn't deny it. She said:

'You read all about it, perhaps.'

He shifted abruptly, but brought the

movement to a lazy close. Would one ever know if he was on his guard?

'I read it. You poor thing. No, *really*.'

'Thank you,' she said stiffly.

He began to look vaguely round the room. 'More brandy?'

The sweetest smile illumined his face, shining harmlessly over Elizabeth. She wondered, with a pang, if it was this that had caught Gwen.

She had another drink herself, whisky. She said, handing Rupert his:

'It was an open verdict, as you'll know. I'm not satisfied.'

'Not?'

'Our brother didn't kill Gwen. There are some things one knows.'

'Then who did, darling?'

'I should like to find out.'

'Why?'

'Because the bare idea that our brother killed Gwen is so evilly wrong it must be seen to be so.'

'The police couldn't do anything about it, darling.'

'I am Gwen's sister.' She had her stroke of genius. 'You, for instance. I think you would tell the police the least that you could.'

He stared at her for a moment, then laughed his thin laugh. His face was thin too, but in a curiously boneless way. There was scant sign of angles, yet it was narrow inside its thin silken frame.

'Of course. Just enough to put myself in the clear.'

'Exactly,' said Elizabeth, in triumph. 'Just enough to put you in the clear. Why should you bother to tell them any more than that?' She leaped a bit further in the dark. 'It's a matter of principle, isn't it?'

He nodded, draining his glass. 'But you think I should – if I can, for heaven's sake – help you?'

'Not that you *should*,' corrected Elizabeth, refilling the glass. 'I just wish that you would. You must be able to.' She handed him the drink. 'I didn't know much about her.'

'I gather that.' He leaned back in his seat. 'Things came and went with Gwen.'

'I've learned that much. Are you talking about yourself?'

'Well, I wasn't.' Again the sweet, confiding smile. 'I was talking about her latest craze, idea-wise. It was on the way out. When she went home, it was on the way out.'

'What was?'

'Ataveh.'

'Who?'

'You're quite right, he is supposed to be a person. A supreme being.' Rupert shrugged. 'Your guess is really as good as mine, dear lady. He is known as a deity.'

'A – what?'

'A deity. A modern god on ancient lines,

with small following in North Kensington.'

'And Gwen – worshipped this god?'

'She wanted to. She persuaded herself sometimes that she did, then the next minute died laughing. *Sorry,* dear. No, Ataveh was a joke. She was beginning to see it.'

'Was it – a secret sort of thing?'

'It was. With rites. She told me about the rites – as a piece of information, she said. But that day she was just in a mood to make one jealous.'

'Jealous? Of a – of a sect?'

'Well, you see, darling, they worshipped *together.* Through the body. All that sort of thing.'

'Oh, no!' Oh, it was worse when it was all imagination. Imagination knew no bounds.

Elizabeth got up and poured herself another drink. The atmosphere in the room was suddenly fetid, and she pushed the window wider.

'Did you ever go?'

'Me? Oh, no, I've had my brushes. I mean, no point in courting disaster.'

'You mean?'

'Well, darling, Ataveh isn't exactly a member of the World Council of Churches.'

'Churches!'

Elizabeth remembered something. She laughed until she began to choke. But as Rupert sprang from his chair she subdued it with a gulp of her drink and he sank back.

'What was that?' he asked her.

'A joke. You'll appreciate my reactions at the moment can be extreme.'

'You gave me an extreme reaction, darling.'

'Is that why you told me about...'

'Ataveh? Probably. Because being helpful generally is against my principles, as you say, never mind the police. Honestly, it was a shock.'

'It was meant to be.'

'You're serious, aren't you? Were you looking for signs of guilt?'

'Oh, I don't suppose so. I know the police have been here before. They gave me your address. I suppose I thought that if you knew about something like – Ataveh and had held out on the police, the sort of shock I could administer might help you to spill it.'

'You're not a mild version of Gwen, you're somebody else.'

'In a way.' Elizabeth heard herself forlorn, and switched hastily back to her triumph. 'Where is this place – you're going to tell me now, aren't you? – you've already fallen down on your principles.'

'It's 36 – 38 something like that, Harbord Terrace.'

'Which?'

'I don't remember. There's a little plaque up. You'll see.'

A bubble of excitement that had started

far down inside her was growing and bouncing to the surface. Gwen hadn't told Wendy Tiller about Ataveh. If she had told Thomas he had disappeared. She was, perhaps, a step ahead of the police at last, standing on the edge of a murky water in whose depths murder could surely breed.

'So you never went with her?'

'Do you mind?'

'How would one join?'

'There you're on your own. But – look at you!' He closed his eyes a moment, acting a shudder. 'Present yourself. It'll do something.'

'And you didn't say anything of this to the police?'

'You're joking, of course. I didn't say anything to the police beyond seeing Jack was all right. And he is, darling. Don't waste time there.'

'Is there anything else you didn't say to the police, that you might say to me now to help me.'

'Not to help you.'

Their eyes met and held expressionlessly. They rose on an instant.

'Thanks,' said Elizabeth.

'Oh, if the kind lady wants to express her thanks, I'd be proud to drink the kind lady's health.'

'I am grateful,' said Elizabeth, 'for what you've been able to tell me. I don't want to see you again.'

She remembered the definition Wendy Tiller had given to the word 'sub'. She fetched her bag over to Gwen's desk, sat down, wrote a cheque and tore it off. Rupert, prowling nearby, was at her side as she held it out, not looking up.

'You can give me the key,' said Elizabeth.

Rupert stared, shook his head and fished a key-ring out of his pocket. He detached a key and dropped it on the desk. Elizabeth recognised it.

'Thank you.'

'Thank you, sister Elizabeth.'

The sitting-room door closed with the merest click, and there was no further sound. After waiting a moment Elizabeth went out into the hall, and then through the flat, to make sure he had gone. He had left a light, not unpleasant scent behind him.

When she was sure there was no one there, Elizabeth went back into the bathroom. She stood and looked at herself in the long mirror, holding out her arms imploringly to the image there, so that Gwen seemed to be begging Elizabeth to help her and it was almost more than Elizabeth could bear. She tore off the wig and buried her face in the basin to restore her sunburned face. When she looked back into the mirror she saw only herself, red-brown blotched skin, long untidy hair, wild eyes. As she watched, the eyes quietened and the acute pain passed.

But the worst was not over. It lay ahead. Rupert had shown her what she still must do. And because Peter King was both perceptive and unable, hitherto, to see her like her sister, she would confront him as she had confronted Rupert and use his reaction to test her disguise.

She spent the rest of the week travelling fruitlessly by day, and in the evenings sitting alone in the flat defying the shadows, crossing names off the C.I.D. list and brooding about Ataveh.

11

On Sunday evening, in the sitting-room of Gwen's flat, Elizabeth got-up-as-Gwen stepped into Peter King's outstretched arms because she was so uncomplicatedly glad to see him. And because his arms had, hitherto, supported her.

But now when they closed round her his hands didn't reassure her in their old solid way. They pulled her roughly against him, and his fingers probed her spine.

When he kissed her, her choked exclamation was only for the momentary loss of her breath. She had learned what his kissing was like before she forced her head aside. She managed to pull herself away from him, perhaps because he too realised what was happening and slackened his hold of her.

They stood a few feet apart, arms hanging at their sides, out of breath.

For Peter King, the vision which had met him at the door and which he had pursued enchanted across the hall, faded before reality. He said:

'You've been drinking whisky – Elizabeth.'

Stung by a just reproach, she didn't notice the pause before her name.

'I suppose I have. Oh!' Her hand flew to her tingling mouth. She forgot guilt in shame. 'You smelt it!'

'Yes. But it was your eyes more…'

They were very bright, larger as her face had tightened and grown thin, and holding now a dancing, almost reckless light that he had never seen, or expected to see, in Elizabeth. He said, forcing concern to overcome desire for Gwen, at least in his voice:

'You mustn't start drinking, Elizabeth. It would be – silly.'

'You're quite right, of course. And doubly silly from me who's so' – her sudden smile might have been malicious – 'ladylike.'

Peter King saw that she had changed through the few moments she had been aware of his desire, perhaps also through the role she had chosen to play. But he still half pretended that she was as she seemed now because she was really Gwen.

She made it easy for him. She stood in front of him, consciously or unconsciously provocative.

'*You'll* have a drink, though?' she suggested.

'I will, darling.'

'And I will. Tonight.'

The word excited him. He said, as he watched her pouring the drinks:

'Why have you done it? For me?'

He had to force himself to ask the question, which meant to admit the masquerade. Perhaps he was thinking that if he admitted it now and got explanations over, he could earn himself the magic of a longer suspension of disbelief…

'I wanted your reaction, I suppose. Then your opinion.'

'My reaction!'

Elizabeth mildly wondered why Peter King laughed so loud and long. She refused to wonder, as a new energy took her walking about the room, why he had embraced her. She was as amazed at her unquestioning acceptance of the change between them as at the change itself.

When he had finished laughing she walked over to him and handed him his drink. They stared silently and curiously at one another. Elizabeth felt herself blushing. She said:

'Oh, well, perhaps your reaction wasn't as clear as it might have been…' She tailed away, and he was forced to acknowledge her innocence.

'It was very clear. I'm not surprised your first victim collapsed.'

'Peter, you've had a chance since I phoned you to think about all that. What do you make of it?'

'We'll talk about it later.'

If they started talking now, it could be a fatal deflector of his bizarre hopes.

He put his hand on her shoulder in the old

slab-like way. His gesture had no reaction on him, because he was thinking of Elizabeth.

'Are you hungry?' he asked her.

'I don't know. I don't seem to think about eating these days.'

'I am. I'd like to take you out before we get down to things.' Dining well, in the right atmosphere, coming back, Gwen flinging off her coat, a moment of mutual appraisal, one small light… Stop it! He'd never put his code into words, but he knew this wasn't part of it.

Elizabeth hesitated. 'If you like. I'll just go and restore myself.'

'No!' He pulled her hand down sharply as it reached her head. She raised her eyebrows. 'No,' he said again, as if reasoning. 'Come and dine out as Gwen. Nearby. It could precipitate something more.'

'Yes. Yes, I suppose so.' Why did she hesitate? He didn't think she was afraid. He studied her anxiously, and saw the explanation come into her face. She was simply tired. Tired of drama probably, of behaving abnormally. Would this mean…? He felt panic-stricken, urgent. He took both her hands.

'You're tired, aren't you?'

Her face relaxed into gratitude. 'Perhaps I am. Of it *all.*'

'I know. Well, perhaps we won't have to

stage any more coups now.'

'We will.' She walked, unteasingly, to the window. 'We'll have to stage the biggest coup of all.' She turned to face him, bracing herself back against the sill. She went on, simply. 'It will be the ordeal of my life.'

Elizabeth's statements could be taken at face value. Peter King felt a fresh stirring of interest. But it could always be reawakened, it would be reawakened. The other could be lost for ever if its climate was destroyed. He said gently:

'Tell me later. Feed me first. We won't go out, we'll eat here – if you have anything going. Have you?'

'Pasta?'

'Fine. I've got a bottle of wine.' He ventured further. 'This evening has a festive possibility somewhere. Don't you feel it?' He went over to her and tilted her chin up towards him, bathing her strained face in a reassuring smile. He glowed, himself, in its false warmth. One of his fingers moved gently on her throat, but his hold was in the main firm and protective. He saw that he was dealing with both twins at once. It would have been a shaming sensation, if he had allowed himself to think about it.

Elizabeth too was divided. She must get Peter King's assurances, and his ideas, on the assault of Ataveh. She must find out if he shared her sense of the importance of

Rupert's revelation…

But his finger moving on her throat fed the new clamourings of her body and her imagination, and she twitched away from him with a sudden smile. It was the dark-to-light of her sister and Peter King, for the second time, felt behind him for support.

'Does that mean,' asked Elizabeth, looking at him over her shoulder, 'that I shouldn't have another scotch?'

Peter King followed her and turned her round. He rested his arms on her shoulders, his hands dangling limp over her back. He said softly, his face a few inches from hers:

'It means that you'll probably enjoy your wine, and your supper, better if you don't.'

'But you'll have one?'

'In a minute. I suspect I'm behind you.'

She trailed 'Y-e-e-s', mesmerised by the insistence of his eyes. It was the first time he had seemed to be seeing her as a woman. It was the most extraordinary thing, though it excited her nerves rather than her ego. The drinks she had had helped to reinforce her strange mood, swinging between passivity and a sort of mindless energy. She looked back at Peter King transfixed, and he bridged the inches between them and kissed her again. He brought her against him, this time, without violence, slowly and steadily. When her mouth relaxed he released it, and slid his across her face, down to her neck.

He meant to leave things there, he really did. But Elizabeth was responding, moving her face against him, taking his hand and guiding it to her breast, her sides…

They sank to the sofa, then to the floor.

Darling, I'm following you at last.

She wasn't thinking of Gwen, she wasn't thinking of anything, but Gwen was there, smiling and holding out her hand. She was at the top of the hill, and Elizabeth was running up to meet her…

'Gwen! Gwen!'

The cry was Peter King's.

Elizabeth heard him, and it was no more than an explanation of them both. Of why he had changed, and of why she had gone over what Gritsy called the slippery slope and not even with love.

'You called me Gwen,' she said, turning her head towards him. Peter King's ceilingward profile was blurred by near sight. But she remembered it by remembering him at the inquests, palely inscrutable. It was as well, oh it was as well, that she wasn't interested in getting behind that inscrutable pallor, in seizing on it. It could send women mad.

'It's as well, Peter,' said Elizabeth, 'that I'm not likely to fall in love with you. Seeing that you've just been making love to my sister.'

She waited in mild curiosity. It took a few seconds for his head to come round. He rested his forehead against hers. There was a small deep sound, which might have been a groan. What he said, at last, surprised her.

'You are the most astonishing woman. I underestimate you minute to minute.'

'How, this time?' She could only prefer his assessment of her to her own.

'I'd thought it would be – marvellous – if you didn't realise. Terrible – or kaput – if you did. Never that – you could know and everything still be all right.'

'I didn't know, when I was… Well, I didn't know I knew.' She shifted up on to her elbow, looking down at him gravely. 'Honestly, Peter, you've been an awful cad. I'm serious.' But she smiled. 'I've never imagined you a cad.'

'We've never imagined anything, really, about each other,' he said, and Elizabeth answered:

'You still don't imagine things – about me.' She pulled the wig off and sent it spinning across the room.

'Nor you, about me,' he said quickly, against the pang of conscience that came with his sight of her hair. But it was true. 'Not as an individual. Think. For you I've been an anchor, a stake in a rough sea. For me you've been distress personified, you've made me feel protective, given me a role. It's been enough, either way.'

He stroked her long yellow hair. He could

scarcely believe he had done what he had with her. It was the memory, rather than her continued presence, which threatened to inflame him again. He pushed the memory aside.

'Don't for goodness sake worry about this, Elizabeth. Worry about the whisky, if anything. I mean that.'

'I know. It's stupid. I don't really need it – as yet.'

'I know you don't.'

He sat up and smiled at her, leaned over to fasten her dress. Gwen's dress.

'Do you feel like cooking spaghetti?'

The pain from the dress was like the early pain, short-lived and incredibly sharp.

'No!' She was smiling.

They went out for a meal. Elizabeth felt almost as of old with Peter, but not with herself. She listened to herself speaking, as if listening to another woman, heard her own laughter, watched her own hands.

They talked business. Peter King took Ataveh seriously. He said over and over again:

'It must help us!'

'I think so. I suspect – what I must do.'

'Tell me.'

'I'm hungry,' said Elizabeth, 'for the first time since I can remember. Although I'm scared stiff. Peter, I must go there. To Ataveh. All my time here has been leading up to that.'

'It was the ordeal you spoke of?'

She nodded, eating vigorously. 'I don't know how one would – join. But if I go along as Gwen's sister – looking like Gwen – it must stir up something.'

'There are some Flying Squad blokes,' said Peter King. 'I'll speak to them. See if anything's known about it. Sometimes they keep things on ice, waiting for something to break.'

'But if they don't know anything?'

'Then they'll start to find out. And so often it's just that they don't know enough. Don't make a move until I've done some sleuthing.'

When he took her back to the flat, Peter King waited in the sitting-room while she undressed and got into bed. When she called him he went in and kissed her good night, on the forehead. She was almost asleep.

'I'll ring you tomorrow.'

She had closed her eyes and only heard his voice, moving away. 'How long can you stay in London?'

'Afternoon. I'll ring about five, before the train. If I can't get answers by then, at least I'll have set up the questions.'

As he was closing the bedroom door she called him. Something she should have seen earlier appeared on the edge of sleep.

'Peter. Do you love Gwen?'

The present tense moved him so much he

came back to the bed. Her eyes were wide open.

'I do love her,' he said. 'If she had lived you would have seen it.' He couldn't go on for fear of crying.

Elizabeth reached up for his hand.

'We've something in common after all,' she said, squeezing the hand.

In the hall he picked up the bottle of wine he had brought with him, and left the flat with it under his arm. He had bought it for his mother and father.

12

Peter King rang next day promptly at five. He said at once, with noticeable anxiety:

'How are you?'

'Very well. Yes, really!' They both laughed slightly at the surprise in her voice.

'What have you been doing?'

'For the first time since I came to London I took charge of the day. I went to the V and A. Bought a dress.' She giggled. 'I even had lunch at Harrod's.'

'Good.'

Elizabeth was amused to recognise that he was a little deflated by her list of activities.

She said:

'Peter, I feel – very well.'

'I'm so glad.'

She thought he had taken it as the subtle thanks she had intended. 'Any news?'

'As good as we could hope for. They're being watched. Some tortured soul called for a vicar on his death-bed a few weeks ago and tried to ease himself of guilt feelings over having consorted with those jokers.'

'And the vicar passed it on.'

'Such as it was. I'm afraid he'd left it too late to be able to talk real sense. Anyway, as a result, one of the blokes I know in the Flying Squad posed as a relative of the deceased and joined.'

Elizabeth began to tremble with relief. It showed her how afraid she was.

'Peter, that's wonderful! Did he have any problems getting in?'

'Don't really know. I've not been able to speak to him personally. But I've arranged to bring him to you next week-end.'

'Oh, you are good.'

'There's more. Next week or so they were planning on raiding the place. I've persuaded them to hold it.'

'So that they can rush in in the nick of time for me?'

'If you still insist on going.'

'I do. Oh, Peter! This means I'll have a friend in the enemy's camp.'

'You'll be all right. And Frank will take us over the course. Sunday evening about eight?'

'Oh, yes. Good-bye, Peter.'

'Good-bye, dear.'

Dusk in the flat, that evening, had lost its power to affect her spirits. Elizabeth cooked and enjoyed an omelette. She felt her solitude, now, as something chosen rather than imposed. She was annoyed, before she was surprised, when the door bell rang.

This was the first time it had rung unexpectedly. In the silence that followed she was short of breath with excitement and apprehension. She put the chain on before opening the door.

A large dark man, frowning, his shoulders drawn up towards his ears, could be partially seen through the narrow gap.

Elizabeth's excitement was justified. She said without thinking:

'Thomas!'

The man's heavy eyebrows rose, and she thought he bowed. A quiet voice, as deep as expected but light, said:

'Since when was the chain employed against Thomas?'

'I couldn't tell you,' said Elizabeth. He had not answered her implied question but her instincts were reassured. She unfastened the chain and opened the door wide, standing aside.

The man's head was down, he started to move into the space she had left, but he suddenly looked up, and stopped dead.

Elizabeth thought that he was very much surprised, although his face was shut, awaiting enlightenment. When they were talking through the doorway he must have thought...

The possibility made her bring up her hands, shivering, under her chin. An expression of concern came into the man's face. He had heavy features, rough individually but not in sum. His head was square, with dark hair which grew up from his forehead before it waved back, his body immensely tall and broad. Elizabeth felt more at home with his solidity than the sapling litheness of such as Rupert Baxter, or even Peter King's slim strength. He said:

'Is there anything the matter?'

'Yes,' said Elizabeth. 'Come in.' She shut the door and walked into the sitting-room. He followed slowly, scratching the top of his head.

In there, she asked again:

'Thomas?'

'Thomas Telford,' he said bowing slightly, 'at your service.'

'Thomas Telford. Do you build bridges?'

'No, alas.'

'I think you might do.' She smiled at him and he smiled back. It completely altered his face.

She noticed the remains of her supper. 'Excuse the debris.'

The gesture of his enormous hand seemed to render it invisible. He looked at her earnestly.

'You must be Elizabeth.' She nodded, tears starting instantly at the thought that Gwen had spoken of her. He looked round the room. 'Where's Gwen?'

Elizabeth thought she had been expecting the question, even wanting it, but when it came it shocked her. She studied him in her turn, and saw that he was so courteously hopeful, so grave, he could never be making the sickest of jokes. She asked him gently:

'Have you been away?'

'Until last night. Did Gwen tell you she hadn't seen me lately?' He smiled slightly, as at a private joke.

'No,' said Elizabeth, 'she didn't. I'm going to explain. But first forgive my questions, and please answer them. Yes, there is something wrong, of course there is. Where have you been?'

'In the Middle East.' He was patient, letting her plan the order of revelation.

'How long have you been away?'

'Three months by the time I'd done.'

Elizabeth paused. Thomas waited, she had his implicit agreement to the priorities she chose. She asked him if he would have a drink.

'Why?'

Elizabeth appreciated the relevance of this response.

'Because I'm going to tell you something dreadful. Oh, I'm afraid I am.'

He went on looking at her in the same grave, courteous way.

'Very well, then, thank you, I'll have a drink,' he said. 'Whisky, if you have it.'

'Soda or water?'

'Water, please.'

As she put the glass down beside him,

Elizabeth said:

'Gwen is dead.'

Remembering that she was a detective, she didn't take her eyes off his face. She could feel him anchoring himself to hers, using his eyes to hang on to it and not be drowned in the sudden quicksand where she had pushed him. He cared for Gwen. He said at last, and she thought of the bellow of an angry wounded bull:

'Gwen wouldn't die!'

'She was killed.'

'Ah!' It was a long-drawn sound, as of partial understanding. 'A car crash.' He said it as a statement.

'No.' Elizabeth moved over to the window. The moon was riding in a brown ring as it had ridden that wicked night. It lit one edge of each terra cotta chimney pot below, making a giant abstract. Elizabeth turned back to the room. Thomas's neck was red, his head thrust forward. 'You must listen,' said Elizabeth desperately and unnecessarily. 'There's worse. There's – horrible. Someone stuck a knife into her.'

He trumpeted:

'Ataveh!'

She ran over to him.

'What do you know about Ataveh?'

He shrugged, spreading huge trembling hands. 'Very little. She wouldn't tell me…'

Elizabeth sank into a chair.

'She didn't tell me anything at all. They think our brother killed her. The police do.'

'Sammy?'

She nodded.

'But isn't he...?'

'Yes. Was, that is. He had a seizure just after we found him with the knife. It *was* the knife. But he didn't do it.'

Elizabeth was speaking calmly but he said:

'Don't go on.'

'It's all right now. But Sammy couldn't have killed Gwen. I've known them both all my life. It isn't possible.'

'Do the police seem to be sure?'

'Sure enough to have closed the case on a verdict against person or persons unknown. They investigated, of course. They have to. The french window was open. No trail though and no clues. I think her life here was a jungle. They put notices in the papers. Didn't you see?'

'I wasn't reading news. Only writing it.'

'Tell me.'

The hectic colour had faded from Thomas's neck and face. He looked much as he had looked when he arrived, except for a puzzled sadness in his eyes which Elizabeth found uncomfortably moving.

'I'm a journalist. News editor. But I was a foreign correspondent in my heyday, and felt like a stint in the field again. My deputy needed blooding, anyway. I chose a small oil crisis, and it blew up and I stayed there and covered it. That's all.'

'We must tell the police about you, all the same.'

'Of course.' He gave her the ghost of a smile, then said sharply, his brows lowering: 'You told me Gwen said nothing to you about Ataveh. How did you know?'

She told him about Rupert as economically as possible. At the end, after a pause, Thomas murmured:

'Fears made flesh. Why is it so much worse then? The facts are the same, with or without specific knowledge.'

'I don't think Rupert meant anything to her,' said Elizabeth. 'Which you probably knew, about whoever it was likely to be.' She gathered courage. 'Did *you* mean anything to her?'

He took a powerful drink at his whisky and retuned his hands to their unmoving position on his knees. He didn't use them at all when he talked.

'Not what I wanted to mean. But in some curious way I think she liked to please me. Part of her got amusement out of trying to shock me – and yet – I used to think sometimes that she said things to me in the hope that I might congratulate her, or at least show satisfaction.' He said shortly, as if this was the least of it, 'She didn't love me.'

'She spoke about me?'

'Quite often. Especially, now I think of it, towards the end.'

Towards the end. Elizabeth thought how quickly he had learned to use such a phrase. Was the glibness of it sinister? Well, the police would investigate. She found she didn't want Thomas Telford's alibi to be broken. She herself had not the slightest fear of him. On the contrary. She was glad he was there.

'Another drink?'

Thomas nodded. 'Won't you have one too?'

'I think I will, now.'

Elizabeth refilled his glass and poured a drink for herself.

As she sat down again Thomas said:

'She seemed especially anxious to get home to you – that last time. I felt – as if she was equating you with safety.'

I'm frightened, Elizabeth.

'Was there anything – did you get the feeling, ever, that there was something specific she was afraid of?'

'I don't know. If I did think so, sometimes, I'd got absolutely nothing to base it on.'

'I'm here,' said Elizabeth, 'because I can't let the implied verdict rest. Sammy! I thought if I tried to get under her London skin I might – find out some things that the police didn't. I have an advantage after all: I'm her twin sister.'

'And, in a way, you look like her,' said Thomas, studying her.

Elizabeth burst out laughing.

'Thomas, we're identical!' She could tell from his surprised face that he hadn't realised it. 'I've got a wig like Gwen's hair,' she said, 'which of course I won't illustrate for you, but if you saw me wearing it then you'd know we were the same to look at.'

'Even with a wig, you wouldn't be,' said Thomas firmly. 'Don't you know – how our features take our prevailing expressions, how we come to look like what we are?' His eyes clouded and he looked away from Elizabeth. He said apologetically: 'That was one of Gwen's theories…' It was the first of many small realisations which would confirm his knowledge that she was dead.

Thomas broke the silence by getting to his feet.

'I must go now. What are you going to do?'

Elizabeth had to tilt her head back to look into his face.

'About you, do you mean?'

He grinned. 'No, I didn't mean that! I'll report to the police this very night. Though of course you'll report me too. You must.'

Elizabeth said, against all her instincts of hospitality and liking for him:

'Report now, from here, will you? I'll get you the number.'

Without looking at him she went across to

the telephone and picked up the receiver. She didn't quite turn her back on him and her hands trembled. Thomas made no move.

She rang Peter King's living quarters first, and it was enough. They found him for her. While she waited Thomas made her heart pound by beginning to move, but he only went slowly across to the window, where he stood looking out.

Elizabeth said to Peter King, without preliminary:

'Peter, I've had an unexpected caller tonight. The "Thomas" that we've heard about. He says he came back last night from the Middle East. Didn't know Gwen was dead. He agreed that I should ring you now.'

'He's still with you?'

'Of course.'

'Good God, Elizabeth. He might have...'

'He might, but I didn't think so. Will you speak to him?'

'Put him on at once.'

'Thomas.' Elizabeth held out the receiver and he came over to her. Her hand over the mouthpiece she said:

'On the other end is Police Constable King, who's our local policeman and discovered Gwen. He's helping me with my inquiries' – incredibly, she and Thomas flashed grins at one another– 'and will tell us where you go from here.' In silence Thomas took the telephone.

'Thomas Telford here.'

From his responses Elizabeth could tell that Peter King was eliciting the facts she already knew. If they were facts. After a longish pause Thomas said, glancing at her:

'If she doesn't object.'

He was silent again, then said: 'Yes, all right, I'll be here. Do you want her again? No? Good night, then.'

He replaced the receiver and came to sit down opposite Elizabeth, who had just decided she was suffering from delayed shock.

'Your Peter King is alerting the appropriate police authorities,' said Thomas, 'and they will be collecting me here just as soon as they can make it. I'm sorry to have to force my company on you at this time of night.' Elizabeth made a dismissive gesture. 'I was asking you,' said Thomas comfortably, as if one aspect of things was entirely out of the way, 'what you were going to do now.'

'Make some coffee,' said Elizabeth, getting to her feet. Thomas rose too, and they found they were clasping hands.

'Thank you,' he said, kissing hers. There was no extravagance in the gesture. 'Thank you for trusting me. It was a tremendous thing. It makes me worry about you in other parts of your private investigation.'

'It was a calculated risk,' said Elizabeth.

He followed her out to the kitchen, where she made coffee and some sandwiches. The omelette seemed a long way off and she helped Thomas to eat them.

Most of their conversation, while they waited, was reminiscences by Elizabeth of the twins' childhood. Thomas was a good listener, and she found she still had those early memories intact. She didn't wonder at all whether she might be boring him.

When the door bell rang she found herself saying:

'Come on Sunday evening – about eight – and meet Peter King. We have a plan.'

'If I'm still at liberty.'

They shook hands, and Thomas went off with the two C.I.D. men who had come for him.

13

A pall had lifted from the days. Each morning now when she awoke, Elizabeth played cheerfully in her mind with the hours ahead, shaping them to her inclinations. Her investigation stood stockstill, waiting, unable to proceed in any but the momentous direction it would find on Sunday. She lived with a constant, steady undercurrent of trepidation, but above it managed to enjoy London: walks in the parks and streets, the purchase of a watercolour, a play one afternoon, spectating people from café tables, pavements, bus tops, sketching them. She completed a commission she had brought to town with her, and despatched it. She drank no more whisky.

When, smiling with eagerness and excitement, a blue ribbon in her hair, she opened the door to Peter King and Frank Jones on Sunday night, she saw the expression of concern already in Peter's face collapse into admiration, and was amused. She felt no recurrence of the excitement he had raised in her the last time they had met, just a pleasure in seeing again an indissolubly bonded friend. She knew and approved that the affection with which he now leaned towards her and kissed her cheek was for Elizabeth the trooper.

Frank Jones stood behind Peter King until motioned forward; small and dark, unremarkable but with a pleasant smile. Elizabeth saw at once that she would like him.

She led them into the sitting-room and took their drinking orders. Frank Jones asked for beer, Peter had whisky.

'How was it with Thomas Telford?' she asked.

'He was easily checked out. He was telling truths all the way.'

'I was convinced of it.' She felt lightened, and realised that since Thomas's visit she had been carrying an extra small anxiety. 'I asked him to join us tonight.'

'Why on earth?'

Peter King was annoyed, and showed it. Elizabeth briefly regretted her uncharacteristic impulse. They were a team, and she should have consulted him.

'I – don't really know, Peter,' she said helplessly. 'I did go so far as to work out that if he was free to come it would mean he wasn't mixed up in anything. I asked him, I suppose, because he was in love with Gwen.'

Elizabeth wasn't sure this was the reason she had asked him. Peter King wasn't sure whether or not he felt appeased. Looking at the slight frown on his normally smooth brow, Elizabeth found a better reason for her invitation, although again she doubted if it was the real one.

'Anyway,' she said, 'Gwen had talked to him a bit about Ataveh. He thought she might be frightened by some specific fear. You're bound to want to meet him sooner or later.'

He felt a fresh interest, which entirely overrode the more muddled personal reactions. 'What time is he coming?'

'Any time.'

Elizabeth spoke carelessly, but felt anxious. Thomas might not come, then or ever. And there was no way now, in law, that she could get to see him if he didn't choose to present himself. When the bell rang she had to make herself get up slowly and stroll to the door.

There was still a frown, and hunched shoulders, both of which relaxed when he saw Elizabeth's smile.

'Enter a free man,' she said, standing aside.

He bowed. 'This is all right?'

'I should have been disappointed if you hadn't come.'

So she would. Already, it was as if a curtain had been drawn against a draught.

Thomas followed her into the sitting-room. The three men were introduced. Frank Jones was tiny, standing between Peter King and Thomas. Elizabeth was glad of the excuse to turn away and get a drink for Thomas, so that she could giggle unobserved. As she gave Thomas his glass she said, looking from Peter to Frank:

'Please tell me.'

Frank glanced at Peter.

'About Ataveh,' said Elizabeth. 'Tell me, was Rupert right? Is it always … does one always have to…?'

'Yes,' said Peter King.

Frank Jones said ponderously:

'A policeman's lot, love.' He had a Welsh lilt to his voice. He obtained a nod from Elizabeth, and started to light a pipe. She noted that Thomas sat in the same attitude of relaxed grimness, his motionless hands on his knees. 'There's one clear leader. They call him the Master. Tall, airy-fairy remote. Berobed in and out of ceremony. Sort of father figure. Called me my child.' Another hysterical giggle threatened Elizabeth. She turned it into a cough.

'Begin at the beginning,' commanded Peter King quietly. He put a momentary kind hand on Elizabeth's shoulder. She glanced instinctively at Thomas, but he was scowling down at his large hands.

'I called,' said Frank Jones, 'and asked them to take me to their leader.'

'Who did you ask?' demanded Peter King sternly.

'Oh, a youth palely loitering in a robe who

opened the door to me, or rather showed his pale thin nose in a crack. I talked – I can talk' – Frank Jones gave the explanatory phrase solely to Elizabeth and Peter King grunted – 'and I picked up one or two words of jargon from that dying fool. He let me in. Well, you'd never expect to see what you do see behind one of those Victorian fronts – a round room right away when you get inside – vast, you know – tiles on the floor, semi-darkness. The youth vamooses on lissom clerical printless toe, leaving Jones...'

'Cut out the poetry, Frank,' said Peter King.

'I think,' said Elizabeth, 'I'd prefer Mr Jones to proceed in his own way. He might make me laugh. Otherwise...' She shivered. She was very much afraid. Thomas raised just his eyes and brows in a swift glance.

'Carry on, Frank,' said Peter King, 'you heard what the lady said.'

'I claimed cousinship with the deceased, and made sure I'd be backed up all along the line if they checked. They did.

'I spun a yarn about the poor fellow's frenzied attempt to pass on the message. So it was, of course – except for the motive behind it. The link made things easy for me, I imagine. With Elizabeth here, it should be easier still.' He paused. 'I was told, in very guarded, high-flown language, what happened in the meetings for worship.'

He looked at Elizabeth, she fancied with a sudden kindness. Thomas seemed to have slumped a little in his chair. He didn't take his eyes off his hands, spread on his knees.

Peter King, pale, angelically profiled and expressionless as ever, said:

'Tell her, Frank.'

Elizabeth felt that Frank Jones was having to force himself into the straight steady look he gave her as he went on speaking, and was sorry for him.

'The room where they meet, love,' he said, 'oh – way beyond the hall, round corners, behind curtains – that room's set out with mattresses. The worshippers come in and wait at the foot of these mattresses, male and female alternately. The only sign of authority is a sort of chiffon wigwam on a platform.' Elizabeth subdued another giggle. She saw Thomas's knuckles whiten. 'When the Master starts intoning the worshippers kneel down, and when he stops – at his signal – they have it off.'

He grinned at her rather desperately, as if the cheerful vulgarism might take from what he was telling her. Thomas gave a heavy sigh, confirmatory, Elizabeth thought, of his fears. She asked:

'Who – who with?'

'With their neighbours. One side or the other. Oh, I don't mean…'

'Stop it, Frank,' said Peter King.

'You're not expected to choose your partner,' said Frank Jones. 'The spirit of Ataveh will prompt you when the moment comes.'

'Is the place lit up?'

She had to ask that question because her thoughts were so horribly visual.

'Kinetically. A globe turns in the ceiling like the old Hammersmith Palais on gala night.'

'What does the Master do – while this is going on?'

'Having just done himself – spear-headed the way to Ataveh is the phrase – he subsides. In all senses, I presume.'

'Don't be so crude, Frank,' said Peter King.

Frank Jones said very gently, leaning across to Elizabeth:

'The new member has his or her initiation ceremony, love. When everybody's assembled, you're brought in by a couple of priests. You stand up front while the Master goes through the ritual of new boys and girls and then, for the one and only time, you select your partner and…'

'Go on, it's all right.'

'…you worship – the two of you – alone.'

Peter King said:

'With fifty – sixty – seventy voyeurs.'

'Seventy-four's the full strength, with me,' said Frank Jones, visibly relieved and brisking up. 'The presentation's tailor-made for us, love,' he said to Elizabeth. 'It'll be lovely, lovely. The lights – you standing up there in the robe...'

'The robe?'

'Just a sort of white sheet, love, cuts out sartorial differences. Your sister – suddenly there again. Oh, it's lovely, the last word in provocation. And time while the Master's talking for nerves to snap.'

'And then?' Elizabeth found she could only whisper. 'And then – the police will be there?'

'They will!' said Frank Jones heartily. 'And so shall I, in the body of the kirk. If there's any unforeseen delay – which there won't be – remember you're to choose, love. You'll choose me. I'll be early and in the front. On the right.'

'You'll be quite safe,' said Peter King, 'if you go. You don't have to go. They're going to raid, something will come out of it. You know it all now. Don't you want to change your mind?'

He gave her no clue, in his calm face, as to the answer he expected, or the one he thought she should give. For the first time since Frank Jones had begun his narrative, Thomas had raised his eyes and was looking at her. Again, she found the pain in them uncomfortably moving. She watched him as she said, surprised:

'Oh, no. I've got to do it. This is the point

of it all.' But she had to ask them: 'Did Gwen really – do all that?'

She jumped when Thomas spoke. He said in a flat voice:

'Latterly I'd wondered if your sister was manic-depressive. The upper and lower edges of the malady make caricatures of the real person.'

'In the clinical sense, did you think?' asked Peter King, dismayed. Myriad adjustments would have to be made to his memories.

'Possibly.' Thomas looked at Elizabeth. 'What do you think?'

Elizabeth shook her head, unable to speak. The idea had never so much as crossed her mind. She leaned back in her chair and closed her eyes, and the tears squeezed from under the lids and ran down her cheeks. She tried to check the heavy sobs that shuddered her chest. One pit opened, to reveal another, blacker and deeper. There was no end to it. Nor to her ignorance and imperception.

The edge of a glass touched her lips. Peter King had brought her brandy. She sipped it obediently from his hand, fastening her eyes on their anxious, wholesome faces. The ugly images receded.

'Can I go there any time?' she asked Frank Jones.

'I went in the afternoon, the first time,' he said, 'and the Master received me. Services are in the early evenings. Not so often. Fortnightly as a rule.'

She turned to Peter King.

'And we agreed I should go as myself?'

'With the wig – and make-up. See the reaction before you announce yourself as the other Miss Hampson. If the Master – or any of them – is involved with anything, there'll surely be a reaction.'

'They may not know she's dead.'

'They may not. In which case there'll be no reaction – unless it's reproach at Gwen's non-attendance.'

'A member of the congregation,' said Frank, 'who suddenly ceased to turn up, could be a worry. Some unaccounted for enquiries were made, it seems, when my "uncle" died.'

'Reg downstairs,' said Peter, 'remembers a man – young, pale, but otherwise unremarkable to the unsuspecting Reg – who came and asked if anything had happened to Gwen. A few weeks after she'd gone to Upper Longford.'

'And what did Reg tell him?'

'That she was dead.'

'Doesn't that suggest,' asked Elizabeth, 'that they must be innocent?'

'It suggests perhaps,' said Peter King, 'that Ataveh's right hand and his left don't necessarily know what each other is doing.'

'It'll cost you,' said Frank, 'thirty-five

pounds.' He counted it out in fivers and gave them to her. 'Entrance fee. Annual sub thereafter, but we needn't worry about that.'

He got up. The rest of them got up, the three men looking at Elizabeth she fancied timidly, as if afraid of what they might have done to her. She smiled at them reassuringly.

'Don't try to be clever, love,' said Frank Jones.

'She never does,' said Peter King.

'I've made some sandwiches,' said Elizabeth, 'and there'll be coffee in a minute. Help yourself to drinks while I get it.'

Thomas followed her out to the kitchen.

'Are you all right?' he asked awkwardly, moving slowly out of her way, and then again, as she darted about the small room.

'Yes, I am.' She stopped in front of him. 'I really am. I'm tough. I would never have thought so, but I know now that I am.'

'Gwen wasn't,' said Thomas, 'although she always thought she was.' A goose walked over his grave, and he shuddered. It was an affecting gesture in so large and steady a man. Elizabeth held out her hand to him and he took it, holding it in both of his.

'I've got to do this,' said Elizabeth, 'I want to do it. At least – not to do it would make nonsense of my coming here – of everything, really, between Gwen and me.'

He turned his head away and then, as if

recollecting something, turned back to her, smiling. 'I see you must. May we meet again?'

Warmth, hope, surged through her.

'I should be sorry if we didn't,' she said. They went on looking at each other until the kettle's roar muted to the near-silence of boiling, and Elizabeth turned away to make the coffee. Thomas carried the tray into the sitting-room.

While they ate and drank, Frank and Peter put on a sort of cabaret act of cross-talk and reminiscence. Elizabeth realised that they knew one another very well. Thomas said little, and showed his unease only in his eyes. She guessed at enormous reserves of compassion and concern. And stoicism. A man like Thomas could feel so much hurt, and stand up to it so grandly, it could be a terrible cruelty to afflict him.

You hurt him, darling, but not near, nowhere near, his capacity for pain.

The three men amused Elizabeth, the anxious way they looked at her as they left her. Peter King, taking her aside, offered, his face faintly pink, to stay behind until she was in bed. She took the offer as being made to Elizabeth, but declined it. She had, tonight, no need of reassurance. When they had gone she rang up Gritsy and told her she would soon be home.

The next day, having put on the silver-blond wig in an unattended café loo,

Elizabeth rang the bell beside the brass plaque of Ataveh, and told the eventual pale face, of which she could just look into one eye, that she was Miss Hampson and earnestly desired an audience of the Master.

14

I am here, darling, I have followed you all the way.

The door slammed behind her, and the sounds of London ceased. They were replaced by her own too-loud footsteps, clacking and crescendoing ceilingwards with each move she made. She stopped, and the priest stopped. She glanced at the hem of his robe. A soft sandal showed. Lissom, clerical, printless. Elizabeth thought of Frank Jones, and was heartened.

She glanced at the priest's face. Pale, thin, expressionless. The eyes were watchful, moving over every inch of her, the head still. Elizabeth wondered about the qualifications required from the priests of Ataveh, what apprenticeship they must serve. It was absurd that she had asked so little of Frank Jones. How long had the building echoed to meek footfalls, been pervaded by a strong Eastern smell?

Elizabeth slid her eyes past the priest, towards dim boundaries. Other priests identically dressed, as neatly coiffed, appeared in the huge circle and as silently left it. Curtains in the dark curves of the walls swung gently from the recent passage of bodies, or of the warm, incense-laden air. Distant, insistent tappings marked the steps of lay men and women, moving singly or in silent groups.

Overhead, the ceiling rose in an elegantly decorated dome, crowned far above by a winking ring of glass. Halfway up was a gallery, from which a priestly figure leaned down.

Hastily Elizabeth brought her eyes back to the priest beside her. He had been joined, soundlessly, by another, as vaguely young, as pale, as close-faced. They were both watching her, and fear engulfed her curiosity.

'The Master?' she queried weakly.

She thought she had counted seven priests. What was the enemy's total strength?

The second priest asked sharply:

'Your name?'

'Miss Hampson.'

Elizabeth held her breath, willing him to ask no more, and both men turned abruptly and began to walk across the expanse of floor. Elizabeth didn't think that they took hold of her, or even touched her; it was as if, as they turned, their robes billowed out and met behind her so that she found herself walking between them and forced to continue walking by the insistent breeze of those conspiratorial robes, despite a sort of shock she felt at the noisy clatter of her steadily moving feet. Instinctively she had lowered her head, and her handbag swung against her stomach from her clasped hands.

They reached, at last, the curved wall and a curtain. One of the priests flicked it aside and moved through. Elizabeth followed him, and the second priest behind her.

Always in line, either moving abreast or one behind the other, Elizabeth always in the centre, they passed beyond other curtains, round corners, along stretches of corridor.

The walls, the carpet where her feet now made no sound, were the colour of stone. In the corners, sometimes, were vases with leaves and rushes, bowls with burning joss-sticks under shaded light brackets.

They came, when Elizabeth had thoroughly lost her way and was a prisoner as surely as if iron gates had clanged behind her, to a door. Heavy, panelled, mahogany, it reminded her that Ataveh was merely the tenant of a building.

They stopped outside the door, and one of the priests knocked. The door was opened immediately, and grudgingly by his mirror image.

'Miss Hampson for the Master,' said one of the escorts.

The voice was as colourless as the face. Not cultured, but not accented.

'What do I tell him?' It could have been the same voice.

The priests, on each side of Elizabeth,

without turning their heads said in chorus:

'What do you want of the Master?'

Looking straight ahead, into the cold eyes of the priest on the door, Elizabeth said humbly:

'I want to find if I am considered worthy to worship Ataveh.'

There was a silence. Glancing at the empty faces, Elizabeth wondered how they exchanged their messages.

At last the priest in front of them opened the door fully and laid a hand on Elizabeth's arm. She moved into the room. Again, she was unaware of a physical pressure, it was as if the touch had reached her brain, which ordered her to walk forward.

The door closed behind her. The priest bowed and glided beyond a curtain. The room was unexpectedly commonplace and secular, an office. There was a desk between the sash windows, with papers on it and a wire tray. The windows looked on to a featureless wall, topped by a tiny piece of blue sky. The reminder of freedom increased Elizabeth's sense of imprisonment.

There was a bookcase on top of a bureau. Normally she would have gone and looked through the glass at the backs of the books. But now she felt restricted and wary. She sat down on an upright chair and closed her eyes.

Our Father, which are in heaven. And which

– who – must be here now. Here, of all places. Must be here. Mr Melbury, I will ask you about this some day. Darling, how can you have chosen to do this? But we never needed to understand one another. That was the least of it.

Elizabeth opened her eyes to greet the presence she felt with her in the room, but she was still alone. She stared at the picture opposite, the only picture there was, a naked woman with breasts to both sides and three black eyes.

She closed her eyes again and managed the whole of the Lord's Prayer, but she thought she was using it as a charm.

'Miss Hampson.'

Elizabeth exclaimed aloud, and heard too much of her weeks of apprehension in the cry of fright.

The Master stood close before her. The curtain across the room still swung slightly. Elizabeth got slowly to her feet and tilted her head up towards his long white chin.

Their eyes met. The Master's eyes seemed far away, too deep to reveal their colour, to catch the light, but their power gripped her own and kept them riveted to his face with its high nose, high cheekbones, smooth creamy skin and sculpted lips. His eyes were his strength. The explanation perhaps of this whole strange structure.

The Master's face was not expressionless,

like the faces of his acolytes, but it revealed only a confident benevolence.

He raised his long white hands above Elizabeth's head, the smallest of gestures.

'My child,' he murmured.

He turned away from her and sat down behind the desk. She was glad of the slight distance this put between them. It was as if a glaring light had softened. She resumed her seat.

The Master sat silent, intent, looking at her still with unwinking benevolence. It was Elizabeth who spoke first, and out of her disappointment.

'Are you not surprised to see me, Master?'

She had a moment of amusement as she heard the stilted phrase. It had been an instinctive response to the Master's style, to his whole set-up.

'Surprised, my child?'

The voice permitted itself a mild curiosity at her question.

'I am Miss Hampson.'

He bent his head towards her. 'So I am informed.'

'Master, have you forgotten my sister?'

Slowly he smiled, a smile of infinite wisdom and compassion. *Darling, did that really turn you on?*

Elizabeth's commonsense asserted itself, ending the possibility of the spell working on her. She moved in her chair to confirm her independence, but kept her eyes on the Master.

He said at last, out of his long smile:

'My child, I forget none of my children.'

'She has died, Master.'

Again he inclined his head. 'We have missed her.'

Elizabeth longed to ask him if he had known that Gwen was dead, but it would be courting unnecessary danger. Such a man would tell her only what he wanted her to know.

'Master,' said Elizabeth, 'I would like to take my sister's place in the worship of Ataveh.'

Her heart was beating in her throat. She forced herself to go on looking into those eyes, as if obedient to them.

There was a pause. Elizabeth managed to maintain her silence. At last the Master said, opening and shutting his hands on the corners of the desk:

'Your sister spoke to you of Ataveh?'

'Yes, Master. She gave me – her belief.'

The Master said, quickly and quietly:

'It is some months, my child, since she left us.'

Oh heavens, oh dear God, how much danger had she overlooked?

'Yes, Master.' Elizabeth listened surprised to her calm response. 'But I have been ill. Her death – was peculiarly terrible. Our brother was involved in it. I lost him too. I have no parents. *The classic victim – how perfect a prize!)* For a time…' She bent her head, feeling her performance merited brief escape from those steady eyes.

The waiting was almost insupportable. At last, to her dizzying relief, she heard:

'My poor child. I understand. But you should have come sooner.'

'I know that now.' She looked up, consciously candid and suppliant. The worst, the hardest, was surely over. 'I tried – from a life's habit – to find help from my church. It failed me. And I had carried always my sister's inspiration from Ataveh … it was only a question of time…'

Elizabeth had a mental picture of Peter King, flashing her sudden pale approval in the courtroom at Great Longford. Another good performance. And she had resigned from the local dramatic society because she had been good only for props and prompts. To apparently grow up, and then to learn so much about oneself! Oh, she had paid, in a few months, for her quiet life.

The Master rose, and came round the desk. Elizabeth got to her feet as he reached her, and they stood as they had stood at the start. The Master lifted his right hand, held it up for a moment, then brought it down on her shoulder. Her whole skin surface crawled at the touch.

'Did your sister,' he asked, 'tell you, my child, of our form of worship?'

Elizabeth looked steadily into the dark tunnels of his eyes.

'She did.'

'All take part.'

'I know, Master.' Her face was firm for a moment and his eyes wavered. He said vaguely:

'The worship of Ataveh is old.'

'How old, Master?'

'As old as life.' She felt it was a phrase he had used many times before.

'In London?'

'Oh, in London.' He waved a dismissive hand. It was a beautiful actor's gesture. 'Ataveh has been worshipped in London for a moment only in time. That is why, as yet, we are so few. But in the East, in the stretches of Asia, man has always known Ataveh.'

Of course. Origins buried among the crowded ranks of real and imaginary eastern gods. It was so easy, so safe.

Elizabeth said:

'His teaching will spread, even in London. My sister was sure.'

'Ah!'

It was impossible to know whether or not he was impressed. His hand still lay without pressure on her shoulder. He said, as they continued to stare at one another:

'So. You do not wish me to explain to you?'

'I already understand.'

She dropped her eyes, and his hand was withdrawn. Out of the corner of her eye she saw it move in front of her in some gesture of blessing. She said without looking up:

'Will Ataveh accept me?'

'My child…'

The white hand came under her chin and lifted it up. She thought of the masculinity of Peter King, his human greed and weakness which she had accepted and understood. With the greatest effort of will she had made since her arrival, she looked calmly at the Master and he kissed her forehead.

She knew then that there wasn't, and could never be, any impulse in him to kiss her mouth.

'Thank you, oh, thank you,' she said, meaning it.

The Master went back behind his desk and sat down. Elizabeth sat down.

'When?' she asked, permitting herself a slight grateful smile.

'We worship,' he said, 'on Thursday nights. Alternately. Such is the strength of Ataveh, for mortal beings it is enough.'

'This week?'

'Next week. But before that, my child…' He leaned over the desk. Elizabeth noticed that his fingers curled and uncurled round its edges… 'there is our worship for *you*.'

'For me?'

'There is an extra service. For you, as for all neophytes.'

'Yes, Master?' If they could only hurry it, so that she could breathe fresh air.

'This first time, my priests will bring you before me when our worshippers are already assembled. You will stand in front of the people. You will choose your fellow-worshipper, and you and he – none but you and he – will worship in the face of those assembled.'

Elizabeth bowed her head.

'You are overcome, my child.'

'Yes, Master.'

'It is Ataveh's will.'

'When, Master?'

The Master opened a tooled leather diary beside him and riffled the pages. Elizabeth saw a few lines of writing, here and there.

'Next week? Tuesday?'

'If you say so, Master.'

He leaned towards her, smiling.

'If *you* say so, my child.'

She looked at him in surprise, then understood. The necessity of her being consulted as to the date of her initiation ceremony brought horribly home what was meant by worship of this particular god. Elizabeth turned her shudder into a cough, looking down at her lap. It didn't matter, thank the Metropolitan Police Force, what the date was, but she pretended to think about it. When she eventually looked up the Master was watching her keenly, with the suspicion of a leer. It was hard to keep her revulsion out of her face and voice.

'Yes, Master,' she whispered momentously, 'Tuesday next week.'

'Come here at seven, child. We will take care of you.'

Oh, Peter King, Frank Jones – Thomas Telford, take care of me!

The Master rose, and Elizabeth with him.

'I will come at seven, Master.'

'There is,' said the Master, smiling across the desk, 'the question of money.'

'Of course.' Elizabeth took her cheque book out of her bag.

'I don't know anything about this side of things,' she said confidingly. 'Gwen never mentioned it – it was the least of it, I suppose.'

'The entrance fee,' said the Master, 'is fifty pounds.'

Fifty pounds. She was paying, as she had expected she might, for her connexion and enthusiasm and apparent ingenuousness.

She leaned on the desk to write, then handed the cheque across.

'What do I pay – later?'

'If all goes well at your initiation – that is, if Ataveh accepts you, my child, you pay thereafter only thirty-five pounds a year. In advance.'

Secure your own corruption! The slogan

came into Elizabeth's mind, but she thought Gwen had slipped it there, with a laugh. Gwen!

She looked up at the Master with swimming eyes, turning her torment to immediate effect.

'Gwen will be glad,' she said.

'Gwen is with Ataveh,' responded the Master, and Elizabeth realised he was the first person she had ever hated.

To her intense relief – the sensation of hate was choking – he pulled a bellrope at the windows. Behind him the small visible corner of blue sky was covered by a hastening cloud. Elizabeth felt incipient claustrophobia, but she must fill in the form the Master handed across to her. Her name, her address, her age, her occupation, previous religious conviction, signature.

When it was ready she said:

'Master.'

'My child?' For the first time Elizabeth sensed something automatic in his response. He was no longer, for the time being, giving her his full attention.

'Master, this record... I wouldn't wish ... there are people without understanding, enlightenment...'

'Of course, my child.' He switched full on. 'There are people without understanding who could damage us both if anyone was – indiscreet.'

They looked at one another.

'Thank you, Master,' said Elizabeth.

The Master put the card into a small filing drawer on the end of his desk. He slipped the cheque inside the diary. There was a knock on the door. The Master called, 'Come!' in a firm cheerful tone, and two priests stood in the doorway. Elizabeth couldn't say whether they were, either or both of them, the priests who had brought her.

The Master came round the desk and lifted his hands above her head.

'My child,' he murmured.

'Good-bye, Master,' murmured Elizabeth, forcing a tremulous smile. She took her place between the priests for the return journey. It was accomplished with the same silence and precision.

The heavy door opened to her. She breathed cold fresh air. Without feeling physical pressure she found herself on the pavement. As she turned round, the door was latching.

Gulping the air, forcing herself to walk steadily and not too fast, Elizabeth moved away. Thomas came in two strides up the next door area steps and fell in behind her. When she had turned the corner he quickened his pace and came alongside her, hands in pockets, shoulders hunched. Elizabeth glanced nervously towards him, and received a shock of joy – more perfect, more complete than all her fears and revulsions.

'Oh, Thomas!'

Tears were starting again and he grabbed her arm, at the same time attracting a taxi cab to the kerb. He said: 'The Ritz, Piccadilly,' and followed her into the taxi. It drew away into the traffic.

Away.

'Don't cry,' said Thomas, 'for too long.' He grinned towards her briefly then sat staring ahead.

'I'm crying for joy. I've never been so glad to see anyone in my whole life. Never! How and why were you there? Not that it matters. I'm just glad you were.'

'I've been there before.' He turned to look at her, tensing, but she was smiling warmly at him, and her smile widened as she met his eyes. Thomas gave a great trumpet of a laugh, throwing himself back in the seat.

'What is it, Thomas?'

He turned to look at her again, and went on looking.

'I can't really tell you,' he said. 'Oh, it's not that I won't, I really don't know if I can. It's just to do with some differences between you and Gwen. And if you think it was tasteless of me to laugh at such a thing, I must bear your displeasure. Putting it at its vaguest and most frivolous: you're kinder to me, Elizabeth.'

'I'm going to use you. I want to tell you

about it.'

'I want you to want to.'

'Oh, Thomas, I'm so glad to see you!'

To be able to express what she truly felt, and to feel an entirely good feeling, seemed the ultimate in bounty.

Thomas took her hand and held it between both of his. The gesture was not the first type of gesture she had received from Peter King, nor the second, but it held the possibility of everything.

'Don't talk just now,' commanded Thomas.

London went past in jerks and rushes. It was four o'clock and the evening traffic was already gathering. Elizabeth didn't mind how long their journey took, or where it ended. She existed, merely, and enjoyed it. Now and then she stole a glance at Thomas; he was always looking ahead, the same brooding peace in his face.

Was he thinking of Gwen, longing for the living Elizabeth to melt by miracle, as Peter King did, into the dead? Perhaps he sensed Gwen in her, as she had begun to sense Gwen in herself. Elizabeth knew at least, beyond any doubt, that she and Thomas were friends and that he would never disappear. It was the first warm lining to her life since Gwen and Sammy had died. She had been afraid that she might not be able to exist outside her shattered lifelong shell. She knew now for certain that she would.

The taxi drew up before the colonnades of the Ritz. Thomas got out and helped Elizabeth on to the pavement. He paid off the driver.

'Tea at the Ritz,' he said, putting his hand under her elbow. 'It's still the best value in Town – for warmth, and comfort, for charm and interest, for service, for the nerves, and for a satisfying nosh.'

The list took them through the swing doors, up on to the curved marble platform, to one of the small round tables.

'Bertie Wooster, looking round in search of relief during a tirade from Aunt Agatha, must have seen this, exactly this,' said Thomas, Elizabeth didn't think he was trying to cheer her up; rather, that he was expressing his own high spirits.

A waiter brought them copious supplies of tea and hot water, making Thomas rub his hands. Another brought a pyramid of small sandwiches, each differently delicious.

They talked lightly, discovering small coincidences of tastes and views. Elizabeth shed the pall of Ataveh with every moment. When he judged, Thomas said:

'Well, then. Rehearse your statement for the police.'

'Yes, I can now. Oh, Thomas, how would it have been if you hadn't been waiting?'

'Unthinkable. Have they – accepted you?'

'They have.'

'Begin at the beginning, as your friend Peter might say.'

'Oh, Thomas, I travelled such a long way from the street. It was almost like a mental journey too – as if I was twisted and turned out of my right mind. They *made* me walk certain ways without touching me. I swear it!'

'It could be. Hypnosis doesn't have to put you to sleep.'

She shivered. 'There seemed to be miles of corridors and turnings and curtains shutting things off – always curtains, until the Master's door.'

'Any difficulty getting in?'

'No. But I was very much under escort there and back. The priests are all young and pale and expressionless. I never knew whether I was seeing the same one again or not. The Master has a quite straightforward room for seeing people – sort of office. I waited ages before he came. And, Thomas, he wasn't surprised.'

'You're disappointed. Don't be. You waited ages?'

'Well, it seemed like it.'

'Did you do anything while you waited?'

'Somehow – no. I just sat straight down on a chair and stayed there.'

'The Master probably wasn't surprised, Elizabeth, because he had seen you before you saw him.'

'You mean…?' She remembered the picture, the eyes, the nipples. 'Oh, Thomas, I didn't feel alone. I'd closed my eyes at one point and I opened them because I thought there was someone there. There wasn't.'

'There was a spy-hole. Well, think, it's the least he can do, in his business. So he played it cool?'

'Entirely. I told him Gwen had passed the message on and all that rubbish. Then I told him firmly I knew what it entailed so I was spared the explanations of – oh, it's horrible! Why does he do it?'

'What did he charge?'

'Ah, yes. Fifty pounds. Against Frank Jones's thirty-five.'

'Depends who he thinks he's dealing with.'

'The money's why he does it, I suppose.'

'Well, partly, of course. Did he – frighten you? As a man might a woman, I mean?'

'No, he didn't. I was afraid automatically at the beginning, of course. His eyes! Then there was a moment – and he kissed my forehead in true father fashion.'

'It's what I suspected. What I hoped, Elizabeth! I've had work contacts in the past with this kind of joker. The greedy onanist, the voyeur. The greed's satisfied in the office – and the rest in that little lonely tent in face of the congregation.' He leaned over and took her hand for a moment as she looked down at her plate, scuffing crumbs.

'Yes, it is vile.'

'Need I tell you any more? The more I think about the Master the more I want to be sick, and it's such a good tea.'

To Ritz standards of timing, a waiter appeared with a tray of cakes. Thomas suggested they each took two.

'When is it to be?' he asked, when they were alone again.

'Tomorrow week. Seven p.m. Just as I am, without one plea. I'm terrified. Thomas, I'm scared to death. I feel almost as if my mind, myself, could disintegrate under the weight of such wickedness. Or I might just stop breathing.'

'Nonsense. Think of yourself as Christian meeting the most challenging of his monsters. Think of Frank and Peter as your guardian angels.'

'Oh, they will be.'

Thomas finished his second cake, and wiped his mouth on the linen napkin. His large features no longer seemed heavy.

'You've got a week, Elizabeth,' he said, 'in which you can do absolutely nothing about the mechanics of the ordeal. You can, though, stiffen your resistance to the evil. You can in fact put in a great deal of good work building up counter strengths. Why, don't you think just one wholesome and lovely image into Christian's mind would have made the dragon lunge amiss?'

'Yes, Thomas.'

'I will see,' said Thomas, 'that you do good things this week, and are happy.'

15

Thomas left her at the lift. When she opened the front door of the flat the telephone was ringing. It was Peter King.

'Are you all right?'

'Yes. Yes.'

'Don't tell me now. Write it out. When?'

'I've got a week's grace.'

'How will you spend it?'

'Thomas Telford took me to the Ritz for tea and has announced his intention of helping it go by. For Gwen's sake of course. Like you.'

For a moment Peter King couldn't speak, he was so taken aback by the only feminine barb she had ever thrown at him. She had had so much occasion to launch one against him in the recent past, and had forborne.

Elizabeth was speechless, too, from the impact of revelation.

Darling, I don't want Thomas around me because he loved you.

It was a terrible possibility, jealousy of Gwen. But she didn't want to share Thomas even with Gwen, with whom, in immediate memory at least, she had been happy to share Peter King.

Need she be jealous? She had said aloud that Thomas was approaching her for Gwen's sake, to see if she believed it, and had stung Peter King so that if it turned out to be true he would at least feel uncomfortable too.

She hoped it wasn't true. That was as far as she could go. But there was something else she was suddenly sure of.

You wouldn't grudge me Thomas. You are so generous. You never collected scalps. I might come to believe your wanting to like him was wanting him for me.

'Elizabeth!'

'I'm sorry, Peter. I've had – a bad day.'

'Dear girl, I'm sure you have. Can you get the gen to Frank Jones?' He gave her the address. 'I'm glad you'll have good company this week. Try not to think of the rest of it before you have to. You've done wonders.'

'Only what Frank did. Plus fifteen quid.'

'Ataveh will topple. At least we know that.'

'Thank God. I don't think I could have done any of it without you, Peter.'

'I think you could.'

'When will you be coming?'

'Not till the evening, I'm afraid.'

'Well, I'll be best on my own, that day.'

'Keep your eyes open meanwhile.'

'What do you mean?'

'I don't know, really. Just – be careful.'

Elizabeth thought next day of what Peter

King had said, as she and Thomas passed a seat in St James's Park and the pale thin young man she had seen at the next table during lunch folded his newspaper and got slowly to his feet.

'What is it?' asked Thomas.

'Nothing. What are we going to do this afternoon. Don't you have to work?'

'I'm on holiday. We both are.'

They walked down to the water. They were part of a small crowd lining it, feeding the ducks, enjoying the late warm sun. Elizabeth tried to dismiss her vague anxiety.

'What do you usually do at lunchtime, Thomas?'

'Exchange news and views with my fellows in a wretchedly crowded pub. Or have a coffee and a sandwich at my desk.'

'Do you have a glamorous secretary?'

'No.' He grinned at her. He looked at her, now, nearly all the time when they were talking.

'Don't you like to get out of town, when you're on holiday?'

'I've just been abroad.'

The seats were popular and it took them some time to find one with room for two. It was good to sit in the sun beside Thomas, not speaking unless she felt like it, savouring the normality and charm of her surroundings, living in sensations – warmth, Thomas's presence, voices of birds and children – rather than in thoughts.

They went to the cinema in Swiss Cottage, a revival they both wanted to see, and had steak and chips afterwards in a small café.

'You see,' said Thomas, grimacing over his coffee, 'you've managed to be happy today.'

'Yes, I have. I've had the nicest day – since the spring. Isn't it extraordinary?'

'Not at all.'

When they pushed open the doors of the flats, a pale thin young man stood aside to let them through. Before vanishing into the night he looked for a moment at Elizabeth with wide, expressionless eyes.

'I'll leave you here,' said Thomas, in the lobby.

Elizabeth let him go.

But the next night, when he drew back from the lift as the doors opened she said:

'Come up. I want to talk to you.'

A pale young man had been behind her when she stepped back from a picture in the Tate. A pale young man had eaten a poached egg on toast at a table for one near the door of the restaurant where Elizabeth had lunched with Thomas, had sat across from them in the tube – if her imagination, by then, wasn't running away with her. The young man, or the young men, had tidy brown hair and grey gabardines. She told Thomas about them.

'Didn't you notice anything?'

'No. But I've been looking almost exclusively at you. I shall notice, now, if there's anything to see.'

'Do you believe me?'

He took her hand and held it against his shoulders.

'That's the wrong question. Of course I believe you. The right question is: were you turning coincidence into significance or not?'

'Oh, I don't know.' She shivered. 'I suppose we'll find out as the week goes on. But, Thomas, how careful they have to be, Ataveh! Gwen's sister coming and looking so like Gwen... *Thomas!*' Elizabeth, unthinking, flung her arms around his shoulders. He held her against him for a moment, then at arms' length, looking at her. 'What was that about?' Her eyes were wide with terror.

'Thomas. *They'll be wondering about my hair!*'

He looked approvingly at the shiny yellow strands.

'So what?'

'Don't you see? I visit them with hair like Gwen's. And I haven't got hair like Gwen's at all! If they really are following me, they'll know that by now. Why did I dress up to visit Ataveh, if it wasn't for a reason? That's why they're following me, Thomas, they're suspicious! But I've got to be like Gwen again – next time – it's the point of everything.'

'If they question you,' said Thomas, hiding his own rising fears, 'you must tell them that as you feel yourself to be carrying on your sister's membership you want to be like your sister, and so on.'

'Yes, that's the only thing I can do. But, Thomas…'

She laid her head on his enormous chest. She was very frightened. Thomas's heart, too, beat loudly. He said, over her head:

'Don't go back, Elizabeth. Don't.'

Despite her terror she had no temptation to obey him.

'I have to go, Thomas. I can't not go.'

'They'll still stage the raid, as Peter said. Something could come of it.'

'They must see Gwen again. It's no good, Thomas, I have to go through with it.'

'Then tell the police.'

'Oh, no.'

'Tell them! Tell Peter King. I shan't leave this flat until you do.'

'I don't want you to leave it, Thomas.'

But she took the receiver when he held it out to her.

As a result, next day Elizabeth and Thomas had an official shadow. Elizabeth noticed only the uniform pale faces of Ataveh, but acknowledged that without the further, unrecognised presences she would have been too scared to go out. As it was, now, she went on enjoying that strange week, raised above time. She and Thomas had to plan their days in advance, because Elizabeth had to relay the timetables over the telephone, to a number Peter King gave her.

They walked in Kew Gardens, on the unexpected green acres of the Tower, saw two plays, ate in a variety of good restaurants. They talked of the immediate future as little as possible, and then only in the privacy of Elizabeth's flat – Thomas had persuaded her, demonstrating the unsullied efficiency of the double locks, that it could not have been bugged. Elizabeth had a rare laugh, deciding she had absorbed too much of current folklore.

On Monday morning Thomas went back to work. The chimney pots below Elizabeth's window were dark with rain, and she informed the telephone that she would stay indoors until the evening. She spent the morning doing housework and washing, trying to pray as she moved about the flat. In the afternoon she read herself to sleep. At six o'clock Thomas came.

The late afternoon sky had been gradually clearing and the evening was rose-pink. Elizabeth rang up again, and she and Thomas went out for a walk.

In a bar where they were the only customers, Elizabeth said, taking a chance on eavesdroppers:

'Gwen will help me tomorrow.'

'What do you mean?' Thomas looked at her in wary astonishment.

She explained. 'She's with me, Thomas. I'll never be without her. Don't you recognise her sometimes?'

She had never seen him so much as slightly annoyed with her, and now he exploded with rage. His eyes flashed, he towered above her.

'What are you saying?'

'Don't, Thomas, don't! What have I done?'

'You're on the way to a right obsession, my lady! Oh, I've seen a few signs. Strange ways of talking about a dead sister. Strange long-distance eyes when you do. Elizabeth, look at me.'

She did so, timidly. He seized her wrist.

'Gwen's dead. Picture her looking down from heaven, if you will. But – not – in possession – of – you.'

'Oh, not in possession, Thomas!'

'Sharing, then?'

Sarcasm is terrible from those we love.

'Please don't talk to me like that. Not sharing, either. And I thought you loved Gwen.'

'What's that bloody got to do with it? Gwen's dead. You're alive, Elizabeth. For God's sake – and mine, and yours – pull yourself together!'

He loves me. Darling, I think you'll be glad. I am! But he doesn't understand some things. Doesn't understand that we talked like this when you were alive, across England. Why not across the other sort of divide? I don't suppose he could ever understand, but it doesn't matter. I'll just be careful what I say to him.

'Oh, Thomas. Do stop being so excited. Gwen and I had a sort of telepathy – you would call it that – when she was alive. So why should it cease now? Don't you believe in life after death?'

'I don't disbelieve.'

'Well, then.' She smiled at him, twisting her hand out of his slackening grip and interlacing his fingers. 'There's nothing wrong.'

It took a half hour for Thomas to completely recover. Elizabeth worked on him with smiles and safe talk until he was disarmed. She was grateful to have learned with so little damage.

On their way back to the flat they had to pass St Saviour's, where she had sat one night in angry disappointment. Now, she wanted to go in to celebrate her private ecumenism, and to pray for help on the morrow.

'Come with me to church, Thomas.'

Elizabeth turned into the gateway, and was dragged back roughly by Thomas and hauled a few feet along the pavement before she could regain her balance. She struggled against his strong leading arm.

'You're not still...?'

'Don't question me. Just keep going. Under your own steam would be preferable.'

His tone instantly ended her resistance. They walked a few minutes in silence.

'What was it?' she asked at last. There would, in the morning, be two bruises on her arm.

'Elizabeth, think! You can't go to church.'

'Why not?'

'What did you say to the Master?'

I tried to find help from my church. It failed.

'Thomas, I'm sorry. Oh, thank you.'

'Don't look back. Just keep walking.'

She kept up into the lobby, into the lift. Thomas came up with her. He put her into an armchair and stood in front of her, frowning down.

'Do you want to see me tomorrow?' he asked at last.

'Will you – take me to Ataveh?'

'Of course.'

'Come at six. Do you want coffee now?'

'No, nothing. Get to bed.'

She looked up at him, laughing.

'Thomas, you were right. I have had a happy week – despite more worries than we ever expected when it began. I think I'll remember it – in the long run – without its attendant shadows … real or imaginary. And I'm much stronger now to meet the dragon.'

She had prayed for sleep and it came quickly and lasted the night long.

The telephone had advised her to spend Tuesday indoors and she was glad to. She finished cleaning the flat. In the afternoon the telephone rang and it was the Fromen Gallery. Could she come and see them as soon as possible?

Elizabeth arranged to go the next afternoon. She might not be up to it in the morning, but to make an appointment for anything that came after her night with Ataveh was a heartening gesture to the future.

Thomas came promptly at six. Elizabeth was ready in Gwen's wig because some remaining insecure part of her wanted to watch his unprepared face. She was slightly ashamed of the impulse, but still gave in to it. And it distracted her thoughts from the events ahead.

When she opened the door to Thomas he remained on the threshold, studying her appearance in an academic sort of a way.

'Yes,' he said at last, 'you do look very alike. And yet everything in your expression proclaims the difference. It's very interesting. Poor Gwen.' He came in and closed the door. 'If she had just had your capacity for contentment.'

She asked indignantly:

'Do you think I'm contented?'

'Oh, not today, my heroine. But you will be.'

They stood at the window hand in hand, in a long silence, both looking out over the chimney pots. The air was clear, and there was a far horizon of towers and tower blocks.

'I'll be going home, of course, after this,' said Elizabeth at last.

'Of course you will.'

The lack of information in his words gave Elizabeth no anxiety. He would arrange things.

'The Fromen Gallery phoned. I'm going tomorrow afternoon. Tomorrow afternoon, Thomas, I'll be in the Fromen Gallery, worrying about pictures (I could never think about anything else, there), and this will be behind me.' She turned to him, putting her hands on his shoulders. 'I've never been so frightened in my life.'

He held her a moment, rubbing the slight roughness of his cheek across her temple. 'It's time to go.'

Thomas had brought his car. Traffic was still heavy and they travelled in stops and starts. Elizabeth clung to the busy sanity of the streets. When Thomas stopped for the last time, with a last look towards her, she got out of the car hardly believing what was happening.

She crossed the pavement without looking back, and rang the bell. The door opened and she was in the hall, without speaking.

More priests, more lay men and women, were moving about. The smell of incense was very strong. Two priests were beside her already, flanking her, inaugurating the march.

This time there was no door at the end of it. They stopped behind perhaps the fourth curtain, in a small room with canvas walls, a table, a chair, and a mirror. There was a row of pegs on one of the walls, from which hung white garments. Another curtain led away opposite. The priests motioned to Elizabeth to remove her coat. Her dress. Her shoes. Her tights. Then they turned away and unhooked one of the white garments from the wall. They put it over her head and it reached almost to her ankles. It was large and loose.

She was sitting in the chair, seeing her pale face in the mirror, amazed at its calm. They put a sort of bed sock on her feet. They went back to the pegs and brought a veil, which they pinned to the wig. It covered her face and dismayed her.

'Do I not lift it?' she whispered.

Well, she would lift it, of course, but best to find out if she could lift it according to the canons of Ataveh.

One of the priests said:

'You will know when to lift it.'

When she was apparently ready the priests went away and almost at once the Master was there, his hands already raised for the blessing he delivered above Elizabeth's head.

'My child,' he murmured.

She looked up, and he took her by the shoulders and raised her to her feet. He lifted the veil back.

'You are prepared, my child?'

The ghost of the leer came and went.

'I am, Master.'

Dear God, it was hard to think of the Metropolitan Police closing in on this miasma, containing it, destroying it. Impossible to imagine them moving in on the doors, the windows. That even now beyond these curtained silences they were ready. Frank Jones kneeling at a paliasse at the heart of the evil, awaiting her.

The Master kissed her forehead.

'You will be brought before us,' he said, and lowered the veil. He withdrew.

Elizabeth stood waiting, unable for a moment to relax from the position he had chosen for her.

Our Father, which art in heaven.

She could get no further than the first line, endlessly repeated. Surely the police were in the building by now, moving nearer and nearer. But how could they know which moment would be her real moment of trial? Our Father, let them be on the safe side...

Elizabeth battled for a second with pure panic, and overcame it. Frank Jones was waiting. One man unperverted by lust or derangement or greed.

Our Father...

Two priests were there, one each side of her. The three of them began walking, beyond the far curtain, round a corner, another curtain, a stretch of corridor, another curtain – how could Peter King find the way, unescorted? – and Elizabeth blinked in a sudden descent of darkness followed by dazzling light. It seemed a large room but its boundaries were lost in gloom. In the ceiling spun a circle of light that flashed a steadily moving pointer of illumination. The lighted places were spattered with black drops from the pattern of the turning globe. Elizabeth and the priests arrived at the foot of a platform, and came to a halt before a tented structure which was all the platform held.

They stopped facing the platform and out of the tent came a voice, amplified:

'We welcome our new-born child, Ataveh, we present her to thee.'

They turned round, and Elizabeth looked out over a succession of pale images, fading one by one into darkness, awakening one by one to fleeting light. Each consisted of white squares, behind each a shadow which the moving finger revealed briefly as a man or a woman. Frank Jones had said ... at the front on the right. She felt no more capable of searching for him than one is capable of studying an audience when one is acting a part on the stage. And she was the star performer. How could she find Frank Jones?

Nothing seemed to move on the indeterminate edges of the travelling light. The veil compounded with the contrasts of light and darkness to impede her vision. Where were they? Where they there at all? Where was Frank Jones?

Our Father, which art in heaven…

The Master was intoning. The service was under way.

'…through whom and for whom we offer ourselves. We, men and women, flesh and blood…'

Her eye lit on a male figure nearby. It looked like Frank Jones.

'And tonight, oh Ataveh, she who yearns to be thy servant…'

This was the end of it, the very end. There couldn't be any more. Was it Frank Jones? Elizabeth forced herself to hold the stocky shadow near her that might be Frank Jones, waiting for the recurring light to tell her.

'Our newborn child, who would worship thee…'

The brief dazzle fell on the dark face. It was Frank Jones. Our Father, it is Frank Jones. But the light passed on and she might lose him. She kept her eyes riveted to where he had been revealed.

'And now, oh Ataveh, thy servant approaches thee…' – the Master's voice was thickening, slurring – 'now.' It rose to a triumphant cry. 'Now, my child, now!'

The light stopped abruptly, flooding Elizabeth. She flung back the veil and stood there, blinded. Beyond her now was utter darkness. She could no longer see Frank Jones. She could no longer see anything beyond her own circle of limelight. She looked down at the pallid backs of her hands, spotlighted, clasped imploringly. There was noise and movement in the darkness. The noise was getting nearer. She threw her head back, waiting.

Just beyond the brilliance a sound detached itself from the other sounds of steps and murmurings. A terrible cry of rage and frustration. It burst through the darkness and it was a pair of hands that seized her throat. Out of the blackness the hands came, to choke her life away.

The dragon. Elizabeth thought, the dragon is in the open, they will know who the dragon is. Sammy, Gwen .. they will know.

She lost consciousness.

16

Elizabeth began to make sense out of the quiet, persistent voice of Peter King. For a moment she thought she was in the little room behind the court room in Great Longford, and that the inquest must be over. There was certainly something she had to learn, some result she hadn't been able to hang on long enough to hear at the due time.

The light above her eyes had a white paper shade. She wasn't in Great Longford. But Peter King was there, and would tell her what there was to know.

'Elizabeth! Elizabeth! How do you feel now?'

She put her hand out, and other hands took her under the arms and pulled her up so that she could see round her without moving her head. Peter King had taken her hand. He was in civvies, with untidy hair. Frank Jones was beside him, wearing a white sheet. Elizabeth looked down at the part of herself visible above the rug. She was wearing a white sheet too. Oh horrible, horrible, for some unknown reason, to be wearing that! She pulled her hand away from Peter King and began to struggle with the sheet, trying to tear it over her head. She began to shiver.

Peter and Frank took a hand each and held them firmly.

'You'll get cold, love,' said Frank, tucking the rug round her shoulders. 'We haven't found your clothes yet.'

'They're here somewhere.'

It hurt her to talk and she sank back, fully remembering. There was a curtain swaying at the foot of the bed.

'Please. Can we go?'

'Soon,' said Peter King.

An unknown man came round the curtain, carrying a bag. Elizabeth looked down at her arm, pulling the white sheet aside, but there was no mark on it.

'How is she now?' asked the police doctor.

'I'm all right,' said Elizabeth crossly. 'Perfectly all right if I get out of this place.'

The doctor sat down on the rug and took her wrist in his hands.

'You've had too many shocks lately, young lady.'

'I'm not young,' said Elizabeth sadly, 'I'm very old.' Tears began to run down her cheeks, and she saw the doctor glance up at the two policemen as if she had just given him the answer to a question. She closed her eyes again, as it was so tiring to keep them open. The warm pressure left her wrist and pressed sharply into her arm. It sent her gently to sleep.

She woke up in bed in the flat. Peter King was sitting beside her in silence. Thomas was in the doorway, leaning against the door-post, his shoulders hunched, his hands in his pockets.

Peter turned round, and Thomas came over. He sat on the bed, and Elizabeth held out a hand to each of them. She managed to smile. She saw on the arm she was holding out to Thomas a red circle in a bruise.

She was wearing her nightdress. There were so many questions she didn't know where to begin.

'The dragon,' she said to Thomas, 'he showed himself. Did I slay him?'

'Yes,' said Thomas gruffly.

Elizabeth took her hands away from them and put them up to her neck. It was painful to touch.

'Where's Frank?'

'Back to work.'

'Oh, Peter, I expect you should be. And you, Thomas.'

They mumbled denials.

'Just tell me *something,*' asked Elizabeth.

'They've all been taken in,' said Peter, 'the Master, the priests, the congregation. Fifteen priests, by the way.'

'Were they all there.'

'The priests were. Quite copious records, well safe-guarded. Should help. All this by the way of course. I've nothing to do with it.'

'Did Frank – reach me?'

'He did. That's all for now.'

'Just tell me the time.'

'Six o'clock, a.m.'

She saw how tired their faces were. Her gratitude made her cry again, more noisily.

A woman in nurse's uniform appeared in the doorway.

'What's all this?' she asked.

Elizabeth's tears turned to laughter. The nurse bustled across, tapped her on the cheek.

'Have we been upsetting her?' she asked the men crossly.

'No, it's all right.' Elizabeth lay back, gasping. 'I was trying to decide – who'd undressed me – all of them or one of them or two of them. I couldn't imagine it. But of course it was you.'

'Well, really!' said the nurse.

Peter King got up.

'I'll have to get the 7.5. This is Nurse Evans, Elizabeth, who will stay with you for a day or two.'

'Oh, Peter…'

'Thank the Metropolitan Police Force.'

'I thank all of you.' It was back to tears. 'It's just so wonderful to be home. Peter, do you remember how we stood in the middle of the sitting-room and hated it, and there didn't seem anything we could do? Thank you, Peter.'

Elizabeth saw that Thomas was smiling approvingly. He appreciated that her first thoughts, just then, were for her fellow victor.

'That will do now,' said Nurse Evans, advancing again.

'I'll come back later,' said Thomas, getting off the bed.

The two men went out and Nurse Evans straightened the pillows.

'May I go to sleep naturally this time?' asked Elizabeth. 'I think I can.'

'Oh dear me yes!' said Nurse Evans.

'Are you a policewoman?'

'Attached.'

Nurse Evans was probably younger than Elizabeth, small and pink-cheeked and immensely crisp and clean, but she talked to Elizabeth as if she was a wayward child. Elizabeth couldn't help smiling as she closed her eyes.

'*There's* a good girl!' said Nurse Evans, moving to the door. 'Would we like a cup of tea?'

'Not just yet,' said Elizabeth drowsily.

The drugs had almost worn off and it hurt her to swallow. The pain kept her on the edge of sleep. Thin pictures of home and Gritsy and Gwen superimposed themselves on her awareness of the room and the bed and movements of the nurse beyond the door. They reinforced her longing to go home.

Home. To walk in the lanes of Upper Longford and go to church every Sunday and work in her own studio.

Yes, but…

You wouldn't take possession of me, darling, I'm too much myself. I'm surprised to find that out. It's true, though.

Work! Elizabeth woke up completely and called out to the nurse. It hurt her throat considerably and the nurse didn't hear. Elizabeth got out of bed and stumbled to a mirror and looked into it. The image danced but she could see the red bruises on her neck and the black ones under her eyes. She needed the country. Despite Thomas, who anyway, if he was deterred by geography, was not the man she thought him.

She made it in a lunge from the table to the door knob.

'Nurse!'

Elizabeth swung on the door, which she had managed to open, and Nurse Evans appeared and helped her, not without an accompaniment of tongue clacking, back to bed.

'We should call if we want something.'

'We did,' said Elizabeth, 'but my throat hurt and you didn't hear.'

She felt sorry for herself, and started to

cry again.

'Poor dear!' said Nurse Evans. 'Well, then, what did we want?'

'I've got an appointment for this afternoon,' said Elizabeth, 'very important.'

'Oh, I don't *think,*' said Nurse Evans, shaking her head, 'not this *afternoon.*'

'Can I make a phone call at nine o'clock?'

'It's ten o'clock now.'

Where had she been? Four mysterious hours which she had thought were a few remembered minutes. No wonder that every second she was feeling better.

Elizabeth got hold of Mr Maitland at the Fromen Gallery, told him she wasn't well.

'Did you want…?'

'Yes, Miss Hampson. We wanted to arrange an exhibition of your work. We are impressed. We think you have a real and individual talent.'

It was incredible, but he had said it. An exhibition.

'When?'

'Oh, in a couple of months. What are your immediate plans?'

'I'm going home to the country. I have commissions, Mr Maitland – things like calendars and book jackets – not particularly artistic ones. They don't take all my time.'

They did, she used to think, in the days when she started work after breakfast and finished at teatime.

'We hope you will do some more original work,' said Mr Maitland.

'I – don't know. It – what you have – arose out of a certain mood.'

She would never again suffer as she had suffered for those pictures. But something might come to measure up to them.

She gave Mr Maitland her home address. He would send her suggested dates. As she rang off she heard the door bell, and Nurse Evans bustling across the hall. She felt cherished. There was enough of her to belong in two places. She walked across the sitting-room without pause or assistance and met Thomas in the doorway. She flopped against him, but his anxious glance showed him she was all right. They sat down side by side on the sofa, holding hands.

'Thomas, I could be on the verge of minor celebrity!'

She told him.

'You'll go home for a while now, won't you?' asked Thomas.

'Yes.'

'Will you get rid of this place?'

'I suppose so. It's a nice thought, to have a place of my own to come – if I come about the pictures, or... But I don't imagine I can really afford it for long.'

'You don't hate it any more.'

She smiled at his percipience.

'No.'

She left some things behind her when she went home. Nurse Evans stayed to help her pack and departed just before Elizabeth did, grudgingly pronouncing her to be as well as could be expected.

There was no news yet from the Ataveh raid, and it would go straight to Peter King in Upper Longford. Thomas took her to the station and said he would see her soon. She felt sure he would, and left him cheerfully.

She was suddenly full of excitement at the thought of being home. And of concern. How had poor Gritsy been, moving alone through the large house of sad and violent memory? Her essential pursuit of the grail of truth seemed in its fulfilment like a self-indulgence.

Peter King met her at the station. He was on duty, and for a moment the sight of his helmeted figure cut out all that had happened since the days when it was the only way Elizabeth knew him. Time was the roughest of guides.

'Peter! Is there any news yet?'

'Not enough. In a few days. I'll tell you right away.'

'How's Gritsy?'

'Longing for you.'

He put her into a taxi. Elizabeth watched him, through the window, getting on to his bicycle.

She could hardly believe, as the countryside went slowly past, that she had been away so short a time. It was a gap, perhaps, that had eased some memories.

Mrs Grice was on the step as the taxi came up the drive, rosy-cheeked, calm, smiling.

'You're better, Gritsy!'

'And you – are thin, Elizabeth!'

'Yes, but you'll see to that.'

There was soon an enormous meal on the table. There were second crop roses and dahlias and the furniture shone.

'Oh, Gritsy,' said Elizabeth, for the umpteenth time, 'it's good to be home.'

Mrs Grice, as usual, asked no large questions, only small ones about Elizabeth's eating habits in London, and the temperature of the flat. Elizabeth didn't know, any more than she had known when she went away, how keenly Mrs Grice had followed her quest.

'We unearthed some horrors, Gritsy,' she said at the end of dinner, which they ate together at the kitchen table. 'The police moved in. We'll know about it soon.'

Gritsy said placidly:

'What was, was, Elizabeth. How can you help Gwen?'

She had suspected that Gritsy didn't understand.

'It's not help, exactly. Except for Sammy's memory.'

'Ah, Sammy!' A cloud came and went on

Mrs Grice's face. Melancholy threatened to descend between them. Elizabeth averted it by telling Mrs Grice about the Fromen Gallery. Mrs Grice seemed interested, to the extent of following Elizabeth into the studio, where Elizabeth set up materials for the morrow.

She would work, and work, and Peter King would come to her with the news.

PART THREE

PETER

17

Peter didn't go to see Elizabeth right away when he got the full report from London. He carried it about with him for a time – on foot, by bicycle, in his fitful sleep. He had never before baulked so hard at a duty. He even avoided Elizabeth in the village when he saw her once in the distance, by cycling rapidly round a corner. It took him a couple of days to become sufficiently ashamed of himself to telephone her and ask if he could go over.

'Is this it, Peter?'

'Yes.'

He had just gone off duty and arrived in uniform. He took his helmet off and looked at Elizabeth with what struck her as uncharacteristic concern.

'How are you now?'

He hoped she was better, the better to take the latest blow.

'I'm fine, Peter. Anxious, of course. Tell me.'

'The Ataveh set-up's rather interesting.'

'Oh, afterwards, please!'

'Let me tell you in my own way.'

She was impressed by the white earnestness of his face.

'All right, Peter.'

They settled into chairs.

'The Master was once on the Halls,' said Peter, 'a hypnosis act. Oh, he can undoubtedly do it. The priests were all young men from drama schools. He got their interest by talk of good money for small works, and their subsequent co-operation by light and constantly renewed hypnosis. Feeding in the religious bit – and the dead-pan behaviour.'

'Did he tell this to the police?'

'He told them some things, as did the priests. It's been pieced together.'

'Wasn't there anyone else involved?'

'Positively not. It's almost incredible. Sixteen men trading so precariously, and with such rewards, on the lusts and lonelinesses of three score and ten. You have to hand it to the Master. His name is Hubert, by the way. Hubert Price.'

It took her a minute or two to stop giggling.

'What's his life style, Peter? Away from Ataveh, I mean.'

'He never was away from Ataveh. He lived on the premises, he just doesn't seem to have gone out.'

'How many of the congregation did they catch?'

'Fifty odd. Assorted cranks.' He flinched.

'It could never be anything less than

cranky,' said Elizabeth firmly.

'Men and women were pretty evenly mixed,' said Peter. 'And Gwen was the youngest of the women.'

'What about the ones who weren't there?'

'We've been lucky. Price kept extensive records. Everyone's been accounted for. That's why we've had to wait.' He hesitated, then took a small decision. 'Gwen was in bad odour.'

'Gwen!'

'It appears she ran away in the middle of a service, and that was the last they saw of her. Oh, they knew she was dead. It was recorded on the card, which had been shifted to a dead file.

'Oh, Peter, I'm glad I didn't know that before. Perhaps it had something to do with me being followed.'

'I don't doubt it. Your card made a cross-reference to Gwen's, with the comment "Surveillance".'

'I was scared when they pinned the veil on – I thought they might have investigated the wig, it was such an opportunity.'

'I think – I suspect they had more sophisticated subsequent investigations in mind.'

At that moment Elizabeth was too impatient to dwell on implications.

'Peter, you're making me drag it out of you. What about the man who – who wanted to kill Gwen a second time?'

'He's a stockbroker, affluent, respectable, married. Aged fifty-seven. Lives in Chiswick.'

'And they've been able to trace his movements.'

'Yes, dear. They've traced everybody's movements.'

'And? And?' Her bright eyes were fixed on him. Her face was flushed and excited. 'They've proved he came down to Upper Longford!'

'No, Elizabeth.'

'But they will.'

Shame engulfed him. He took her hands.

'They proved he didn't. They've proved nobody did. Not one of those people involved with Ataveh – not the Master, nor the priests, nor one member of the congregation, can be suspected of being anywhere near Upper Longford the night Gwen died.'

She said pleadingly:

'But he tried to kill me.'

'He's spoken quite fully. Gwen apparently, after – worshipping with him a few times, refused to accept him as a – as a partner again. It wasn't religion any more for him, he was simply besotted with her. He was helpless when Gwen ceased to appear. There was no access to Ataveh's records, and he didn't even know her name. He didn't know she was dead. When she reappeared, standing lit up in front of him – "taunting him" – he lost his head. That's all. Perhaps he would have been guilty of murder if Frank Jones hadn't been there, but he wouldn't have had two crimes to answer for.'

'How do you know?'

'We know,' said Peter gently, 'that he was in France the night Gwen died.'

'So it was somebody else,' she said impatiently, 'another member of the congregation.'

'I've told you, no. Not a member of the congregation, nor a priest, nor the Master. Everyone connected with the place is accounted for.'

She went on looking at him, and it took a few seconds for the last flicker of hope to die out of her eyes. Peter had to look away, as once before in this room with Elizabeth. At last she said, in a small hard voice:

'So it's all been for nothing. All – that.' She laughed, the unpleasant sound he hadn't heard for a while.

'In a sense. But it's shown us, perhaps, how complex it all is. I mean, it's made me feel, at least, even less likely to believe the circumstantial evidence.'

'It's not enough for what I've suffered,' said Elizabeth. She got up and walked over to the window.

'Elizabeth,' said Peter eagerly, watching her straight back and tilted chin. That was the attitude in which she always met a blow, as he had learned. 'I can't tell you why, but

… I've never forgotten my own puzzle – do you remember? – something wrong with the screams? We haven't – naturally – thought lately about what actually happened that night. We'll get back to wrestling with basics. We won't give up.'

He had expected to find himself telling her to forget it all, concentrate on work and friends, but he meant what he was saying.

'Oh, I'll give up,' said Elizabeth. 'I couldn't take any more disappointment.'

'I think,' said Peter, 'we might ask Mrs Grice to join us.'

'Yes, of course. I'm being selfish. I'm sorry for myself.'

Before going to call Gritsy, Elizabeth went over to Peter and stood in front of him. He got up.

She said listlessly. 'This doesn't take in any way from what you've done for me – for us.' She tried to smile. 'It was a marvellous team. But it's disbanded. Don't pretend.' She leaned forward and put her cheek against his. He held her for a moment in the old way. Elizabeth.

Mrs Grice was moving about the kitchen. She smiled towards Elizabeth, then stopped dead at sight of her stony face.

'Will you come and join us, Gritsy?'

'Do you want some tea or coffee, pet?'

'Not just now.'

They went into the sitting-room and Mrs

Grice sat down.

'Well, Mr King, are your investigations over?'

'They are, Mrs Grice, and they've led nowhere. Nowhere at all. The mystery is still a mystery.'

'It wasn't Sammy,' said Mrs Grice. She glanced at Elizabeth and Elizabeth met her concerned eyes.

'Yes, Gritsy,' she said, 'I've failed. I've never been so unhappy in my whole life.'

Peter knew this wasn't true but, watching Mrs Grice, he saw her concern concentrate into an agonised pity.

'Never so unhappy,' repeated Elizabeth.

Peter's head swam. He looked at his watch and got up quickly.

'I must go!'

The other two got up. Mrs Grice smiled and left them. Peter said to Elizabeth:

'Come to the gate with me. Slip a coat on, its fine but there's a cold wind.'

'I don't need a coat.'

'Do as I say!'

She collected an anorak from the cloakroom. To her surprise, when he had helped her into it, Peter suddenly produced her handbag, which she had left in the sitting-room, and thrust it over her arm.

'What on earth?'

He whirled her out through the front door, leaving it on the latch. He hissed in her ear:

'I beg you not to resist me, or appear to be arguing. Walk of your own accord to the gate.'

Elizabeth felt she was accustomed to the process of sudden and inexplicable moves. But she had thought the time for them was over.

She walked obediently beside Peter to the front gate.

Kim was there on his long lead. He embraced Elizabeth.

'Why on earth didn't you bring him in?'

'I thought his absence, somehow, might bring me more quickly to the unhappy point. I'm afraid it didn't.'

'Peter, what's the point now?'

'Walk down the lane with me.'

Elizabeth shook her head, but followed him through the gate. The dog surged joyfully ahead, and there was no chance of talk for several seconds. The house and the church disappeared over the high hedge.

'Peter, what is it?'

'I want you, Elizabeth, first of all,' said Peter rapidly, 'to promise you'll do what I ask you, without arguing. Just take my word that it's important. Right?'

'Well – all right, then.'

She was too dispirited to argue, anyway.

'I want you to come with me to Jenny Kirk's tea-room and sit down to tea – on your own. I'll be leaving you there. If you haven't heard from me by the time she closes – an hour, I suppose, it's nearly five now – go along to the White Rose. Sit down there with a drink, and you *will* hear from me. Will you feel all right on your own there?'

'In Upper Longford? Of course. But, Peter – what's it all about? Can't you tell me? And I should say something to Gritsy, at least. She doesn't even know I've left the house!'

'Don't worry about Gritsy, I'll let her know. Elizabeth, promise me you won't do *anything* or say anything to *anybody*. Just sit – first in the tea-room and then in the pub. Promise me!'

'All right, Peter, I promise. But can't you tell me anything?'

'Not yet. Perhaps when I see you next I'll tell you a lot. Meanwhile – please just do as I say.'

'All right.'

She spoke carelessly. She was still too deeply disappointed to be properly curious.

They continued in silence until the lane gave without jar on to the village street. Peter left Elizabeth unlatching the door of Jenny Kirk's tea-room. Through the thinly steamed windows he could see points of light and trays of homemade cakes and female heads. He pressed her hand.

'Wait for me!'

She smiled with her mouth alone, and went inside.

Peter carried on to the post office, pulled a face at his photograph, and asked Mrs Phillips if he could use her private telephone. The public telephone was exactly what it said.

After he had made a call he took Kim by the lead and set off back up the hill. Mr Melbury was in the churchyard, and they talked for a moment over the hedge. Peter was impatient at being delayed, but was the sort of person who always made the best of an enforced detour. He asked Mr Melbury if he had seen Elizabeth since her return.

'She was in church on Sunday,' said the vicar, 'and we have arranged to have a little talk. One day this week, I think. I can't remember which day, I'm afraid, without recourse to the diary.'

'Don't let her put the appointment off,' said Peter, 'and please persist in keeping an eye on her.'

He went into Melbury Grange by the back gate. Kim put on a spurt as they entered the yard, and Peter let the lead go. When he put his head round the open kitchen door, Mrs Grice was fondling the dog's head. Elizabeth's cat, on its chair, had wide-open yellow eyes.

Mrs Grice went across to the biscuit tin.

'Sit down, Mr King,' she said over her shoulder.

Peter sat down at the table and put his

helmet in front of him. It was hard to believe that this was the same world in which he had done this before, and learned that there was a twin sister. He was glad there was no time to be more than fleetingly nostalgic.

'Tea, Mr King?' asked Mrs Grice, warming the brown pot.

'Thank you, Mrs Grice.'

She brought the pot and two mugs to the table, and sat down across from him. She looked at him thoughtfully.

'You said you were in a hurry, Mr King.'

'I am, Mrs Grice.'

She poured their tea. She remembered how he liked the milk and sugar. They sat in silence, sipping, looking at each other over the steaming rims.

Peter said at last:

'Elizabeth isn't really unhappy, Mrs Grice.'

'You know that, do you, Mr King?'

Her expression was as unrevealing as ever, but her eyes hardly left him.

'I know it. She's had a disappointment, oh, yes. But good things happened to her in London. Not least a break for her work.'

'Then you've no need to worry about her, Mr King.'

'Oh, I shan't, Mrs Grice. She's down in the village, by the way.'

Mrs Grice moved her hand sharply and her teaspoon fell on to the table top. She felt for it and picked it up again without taking her eyes off Peter. In the silence that followed he heard Kim scratching violently, the cat sigh, the kitchen clock seem to crescendo its fat heavy ticking. He forced himself to stay silent and at last Mrs Grice said:

'Why is Elizabeth in the village, Mr King?'

'Because I sent her there.'

'Is she intending to be back for her supper?'

'I asked her to wait until she heard from me. You love her very much don't you, Mrs Grice?'

The brown eyes sparkled with a rush of tears.

'I loved them both as my own, Mr King.'

'And Gwen really *was* unhappy.'

She leaned forward eagerly. She was sitting with her back to the open staircase in the corner of the kitchen. Peter was facing it. He glanced up quickly, then away again. Mrs Grice didn't seem to notice.

'It was her temperament, Mr King. At war with herself from the very start. I thought – I thought Alan would have made things different, and perhaps he would, but he left her. He made things worse. After Alan ... she got into some real bad ways and bad company. Disgusting, Mr King!' Mrs Grice's eyes glowed with excitement. 'She used her body for photographs. Naked. I found some. A Hampson! How could she be happy?'

'So you helped her out, Mrs Grice. Tell me about it.'

They looked at each other again in silence, for a long moment, and Peter sensed a tension going out of his adversary. She ended the silence with a heavy sigh.

'I knew as soon as I saw her, last time she came home, that she was – what can I call it? – hurt, Mr King. Hurt beyond hope. Life hurt her. To be alive, for her, by then, was to be unhappy. And she told me. In so many words she said: "Gritsy," she said, "I'm so horribly unhappy." I hadn't been entirely sure up till then, but I'd picked up the stiletto in case. We smiled at each other as I slipped it in. It was like handing her a flower. It went in so easily. She never lost that smile. She never had a moment of doubt. Not a *moment*, Mr King,' said Mrs Grice accusingly, as if he was proposing a contradiction, 'she was grateful to me. How could I have refused her?'

He didn't try to answer that question.

'You were very clever,' he said, 'afterwards.'

She shrugged her shoulders. 'It didn't really matter for me. But I had Elizabeth to look after. And Sammy – I thought.' Her face clouded and crumpled. Peter realised she had always lost her composure when talking of Sammy, since his death. It was the one thing she hadn't envisaged. 'Sammy was happy,' she said indignantly. 'Nothing should have happened to Sammy. He wasn't happy as a small child, Mr King, nobody wanted him. But after the accident it didn't matter what happened to him – outside – he had his happiness within.'

Peter swung dizzily away from this latest possibility. He couldn't contemplate it – at any rate not yet, not now.

'So what did you do then, Mrs Grice?'

'I went to unlock the french window, so that it would look as if someone had come in from outside. It was unlocked already. Then I wiped the handle of the knife with my handkerchief. Then – I wanted to stay and watch her face, Mr King. It was so peaceful and happy. Gwen hadn't looked like that since she was a young thing – with Alan – and not often then. I sat down beside her and stroked her hair.' Peter's skin crawled. He glanced up again at the shadows above the stairs. 'I was sitting there, the two of us so happy and peaceful, and Sammy came in, Mr King! I suppose he couldn't sleep, poor lamb, sometimes he couldn't sleep. He came stumbling in, and across to me, and then he saw Gwen, and something happened to him, Mr King. You saw him, yourself! I jumped up to try and comfort him and he just pushed me away. He was very strong, Mr King, and I fell over and when I picked myself up he'd pulled the little knife out of her and was waving it about. There hadn't been any blood when I gave it to her – so *quietly,* Mr King – but there was a bit now on Sammy from the knife and the savage way he'd pulled it out. I didn't know what he was going to do, Mr King. I'd never seen him look like that, never – dancing about and beside himself. Angry! He frightened me to death. I'm afraid my nerve went. I just heard myself screaming and screaming.'

'That's it!' Peter banged at his forehead with the palm of his hand.

'What is it, Mr King?' asked Mrs Grice solicitously. She poured him another mug of tea.

'Those screams. They've puzzled me all along, but I didn't know why. Why should I think there was something about the screams that didn't fit? Of course I thought – we all thought – they were Sammy's screams. But somewhere I couldn't accept that. Why couldn't I accept it?' She was listening to him with calm courtesy. 'Because, Mrs Grice, *they were not the screams of a mental defective.* They were the screams of a normal person, badly scared.'

A normal person? A person, at least, who knew what she was doing.

Mrs Grice waited a second, as if seeing whether or not he had finished.

'After I'd screamed, Mr King, I realised what it meant – Elizabeth would hear me. I thought that … if Sammy was found there, with the knife … nothing – cruel – could be done to Sammy, he was proof against the outside world – and he and Elizabeth would need me.'

For further service in due course?

'You thought very quickly, Mrs Grice.'

She said complacently:

'I've always been good in an emergency, Mr King.'

'So what did you do then?'

'I went out of the studio and into the kitchen, and up these stairs.' She turned and pointed upwards. Peter knew how fast she could move. 'And straight on to the landing and to the main stairs. Elizabeth had reached the bottom as I reached the top. The rest you know.'

'Yes.' He drank some tea. Mrs Grice poured herself another cup and started to sip it.

'What are you going to do now, Mr King?' she asked him.

'What can I do?' he said. 'You know what I must do.'

'There are just the two of us, Mr King.' She looked at him with wide, tranquil eyes.

He shook his head and pointed to the stairs, then to the back door, still ajar. He said very gently:

'Would you like us to leave you alone for a few minutes? It's all been so quick for you.

And it will be the last time you'll be alone for a long while. We could do that.'

She said placidly:

'Thank you, Mr King, I'd appreciate it.'

Peter got up, took his helmet and Kim's lead, and went out into the hall. He walked up and down. He picked up and examined a photograph of two identical smiling little girls. He looked through the red-stained glass of the front door on to a bloodwashed world. His watch told him only five minutes had gone by when he heard a heavy thud and immediately afterwards a man shouting and the sound of boots on stairs.

He sprang into the kitchen just as Police Constable Waterman, leaping two at a time down the back stairs, reached Mrs Grice. She had fallen against the foot of the stairs on her side, huddled up as if hiding her deed. Another policeman came in through the back door.

'I couldn't see,' said Police Constable Waterman tragically, 'and you told me not to move till you said.'

'I didn't want you to see,' said Peter, bending over and tidying a loose strand of grey hair. It looked as if she had used a kitchen knife.

'You meant this to happen!'

'Don't say that. I thought she might prefer it. She wouldn't have been happy any longer. I gave her the chance, and she took it.'

'She's dead,' said Police Constable Edwards. Police Constable Waterman was taking notes.

'Hang on a minute, will you?' said Peter. He went across the kitchen and soothed the terrified cat, pressed up with enormous eyes and tail against the back of its chair, then went through to the hall.

He rang up Elizabeth at the White Rose and told her he was coming to fetch her.

He rang telegrams and sent a message to Thomas Telford, care of his newspaper. 'Come down as soon as possible to Melbury Grange. Peter King.'

Gwen was dead but Elizabeth was alive.

Thomas was the lucky one.

He put his head into the kitchen.

'The telephone's in the hall. Get things moving. I'll be at the White Rose if you need me. Let me know there, Tony, when everything's cleared away.'

He took Kim's lead and went off down the hill to Elizabeth.

The publishers hope that this book has given you enjoyable reading. Large Print Books are especially designed to be as easy to see and hold as possible. If you wish a complete list of our books please ask at your local library or write directly to:

Dales Large Print Books
Magna House, Long Preston,
Skipton, North Yorkshire.
BD23 4ND